A TRAIN IS LATE THIS CHRISTMAS

CP WARD

BY CP WARD

The Delightful Christmas Series

I'm Glad I Found You This Christmas

We'll have a Wonderful Cornish Christmas

Coming Home to Me This Christmas

Christmas at the Marshmallow Cafe

Christmas at Snowflake Lodge

Christmas at Log Fire Cabins

A Stranger Arrives this Christmas

A Train is Late This Christmas

The Glorious Summer Series

Summer at Blue Sands Cove

Summer at Tall Trees Lake

Summer at Harbour View House

The Warm Days of Autumn Series

Autumn in Sycamore Park

Autumn at the Willow River Guesthouse

Autumn in Sunset Harbour

Autumn at the Oak Tree Cafe

A TRAIN IS LATE THIS CHRISTMAS

1

———

AN UNEXPECTED CHANGE IN THE WEATHER

COUNTRYSIDE LIFE WASN'T the magazine Julia Adams would have chosen given a little more time, but it had been closest to the tills and therefore would have to do.

She had made the train, though. That was the important thing.

As the two-carriage commuter trundled out of Brentwell Station, Julia allowed herself to relax, leaning against the window as lines of houses passed by, the first flutters of an early snow flicking against the glass, where the flakes melted and combined into little streamers to be buffeted sideways by the wind as the train picked up speed.

She would be home soon. Her parents would be there, and perhaps her sister's family would already have arrived. Once the initial jokes about her showing up alone yet again were out of the way, Julia would enjoy eating and drinking herself silly, playing games with her nieces and nephews—two of each last year, but it wasn't impossible that number five could show up over Christmas—and watching too much bad Christmas television.

She sighed. So nice to have two weeks off work. Mary next door was looking after Mittens, her cat, and promised to go in and check that none of the pipes had burst if the big freeze the weather forecast had mentioned actually happened. She had noticed the local bookies offering pretty good odds on "Will it actually snow this Christmas?" on a signboard outside the shop, but even though Julia was expecting the usual rain in Olive Hill, had she been a gambler she might have been tempted with a flutter.

Instead, she contented herself with flicking through the pages of *Countryside Life* dreaming of kitchens, living rooms and bathrooms that she would never be able to afford.

Twenty minutes later, the train came to a stop in Willow River, where about half the passengers disembarked. Out on the platform, snuggly dressed relatives and loved ones came forward with open arms to greet the alightees, patting shoulders, offering warm embraces, taking suitcases and leaning inwards in that way where any conversation was welcome, even a boring monologue about the train journey from Brentwell.

Julia smiled. It was what the Christmas holidays were all about. Perhaps Mum and Dad would be waiting at the station when she got to Olive Hill? It was only a short walk and Becky would have passed off her clan for Barbie marathons and games of Connect 4, so it wasn't likely, but maybe, just maybe. Like they had in the old days, when she came back from university for a visit, waiting for her as though they hoped she'd never leave again.

Which of course, she always had.

A sudden wave of nostalgia washed over her, and she gave one of those awkward gasp sobs that was out before she could stop herself, as though a balloon stuck in her throat had decided to set itself free. A young man sitting in a window seat further up the train looked up from a newspaper and gave her a frown and a forgiving smile, while a boy playing a Nintendo Switch in the seat across the aisle stifled a snigger and turned to stare pointedly out of the window. Julia smiled back at the man and forced a fake cough to try to cover it, but there was no denying how she felt.

Nearly thirty-five now, and time was moving on, slipping slowly past like the railway sleepers beneath the wheels of the train.

Which ... now that she thought about it, weren't moving all that fast.

She glanced out of the window, wondering why they appeared to be going so slowly. They were going through a patch of farmland, but she barely recognised it now that the snow had picked up and covered everything in a blanket of white. It really was a blizzard, the like of which she hadn't seen since she was a child. Perhaps it was global warming, even if that was a bit of an oxymoron, considering how chilly the carriage was getting.

She climbed half out of her seat and looked up the carriage. Most of the seats were empty but a few kids were leaning against the windows, muttering vague threats about snowball fights and fort battles to come in the morning when the skies would likely have cleared and the school holidays were officially underway. A couple of parents ordered them to sit down, lower their voices, mind the other passengers.

Julia had just sat back down when the train came to a grinding halt. The pneumatics hissed, and the rails gave a lazy squeal. A burst of loud static came from a speaker overhead, and then the driver's voice said, 'I do apologise for the delay. We'll be moving again in a moment. Bear with us, please.'

Further up the carriage, people were starting to

speculate. Julia caught the eye of the young man in the window seat and he gave her a shrug and a quizzical shake of the head. The boy opposite, buried in his game, didn't appear to notice the stoppage.

Outside, the snow was dumping down.

'Never seen nothing quite like this,' said an old man about halfway up the carriage, standing up to make his pronouncement as though the carriage had suddenly transformed into a soapbox stage. 'Not since sixty-three. Came down in buckets that year, as though someone up there was scooping the stuff. Thick as ice-cream, though didn't taste quite the same.'

'Dad, please sit down,' came a woman's voice, her identity hidden by the seats.

'Couldn't leave the village for a week that year,' the man continued. 'We kids didn't want it to end. Went out there with shovels and built a barricade across the only road into the village. Silly old tractor went into a pond by mistake, thinking 'twas the thoroughfare—'

'Dad, you'll start scaring people!'

'Best Christmas ever. Built a big old bonfire in the village square and danced round it 'til midnight. 'Twas where I met your mother, 'twas. Pub's cellar was running empty … good times. We had all that cheering and stuff when the clock ticked round, and then we went back home for some sherries and a little cuddle up by the log fire—'

'Dad, please!'

'What happened, Grandad?'

'Ah, best save that last bit for when you's a little older,' the old man said with a chuckle. 'But your uncle showed up nine months later, and your mother a couple of years after that. Can't beat the magic of a good snowstorm.'

Julia smiled, but as she looked out of the window, she

found her fingers tapping nervously on the armrest. While she had nothing against snow, the thought of getting stuck on a train overnight certainly didn't appeal—

With a lurch it began to move forward, and Julia let out a sigh of relief. The man in the window seat smiled and gave her a thumbs' up. From the seats in front came a series of contrasting cheers and boos.

'We apologise for the delay,' came the driver's voice through the speaker. 'We're currently ten minutes behind schedule. I can't promise we'll make that up in this weather, but we're not expecting any more delays. Next stop, Bathwater, in twelve minutes.'

Julia leaned back in her seat, a strange feeling washing over her. Hadn't a part of her been excited about the thought of getting stuck? What would they all have done? She had a bottle of water and a packet of steak flavour McCoy's in her bag, but other than that, nothing. Would the train's heating have stayed on, or would it have got really cold? She glanced up at the young man further down the aisle. He was probably in or close to his thirties, and attractive enough that she could daydream about a romantic encounter. He was reading his newspaper again now. A *Daily Express*, she thought. What would Dad say that made him? A Liberal? A Conservative? Or had he, like she, just picked up whatever was closest as he ran for the train?

She opened her copy of *Countryside Life* again, tilting it slightly so he would be able to see the title. Perhaps he would think she was an interior designer or an architect, rather than an insurance claims administrator, a job which, for the most part, involved tapping numbers into a screen all day long.

When she glanced up again, he was not looking at her,

but wore a slight smile. Perhaps he understood the game. Or perhaps he was looking at the jokes page.

Did the *Daily Express* have a jokes page?

Dad would have said something like, 'That whole paper's a joke.' Or was that the *Daily Mail*?

Outside the snow seemed even heavier than before. It was getting dark now, but she could only tell from the shadow that seemed to back the snowfall, as she could no longer see anything beyond the snow. They were coming up for Bathwater, a drab little place no one ever visited which was famous only for a pie factory, but the flat farmland that surrounded it was hidden behind the snow. Further up the train, the kids began to whoop as a sudden gust of wind turned the snowfall towards the train, buffeting the windows so hard it sounded like fingers drumming on the glass.

'Bathwater,' announced the driver. 'Bathwater in two minutes.'

Nearly home. Three more stops, she thought, although until her car had failed the MOT she had usually driven down from Brentwell. Fourteen years on since graduating, and she felt like a student again, just one who was still doing an entry level job and who couldn't handle hangovers anymore.

The train pulled in at Bathwater, and a couple of people got off, sighing as they did so, as though it were a regrettable chore. Then the train pulled out of the station again, leaving Bathwater behind. Olive Hill was much nicer, and the thought of being home made Julia smile, even if she would be inundated with game requests by her sister's lot within seconds of walking through the door. Still, she had gone last Christmas unbeaten at Guess Who?, and had even once managed to beat her dad—a self-proclaimed master—at Jenga. However, the kids were growing up, and it wouldn't be long before she could no longer pretend to miss easy wins at Connect 4 in order to give them a chance, and would find herself on the losing side. And once that happened, once she could no longer compete, what was the point? What was the point of coming home at all? Fifty and a spinster, whitewashed at memory games, always the one to make the Jenga tower fall, she might as well be in the ground already—

The train's brakes squealed, and she lurched forward, nearly headbutting the back of the seat in front.

'My apologies,' came the driver's voice through the speaker. 'Unfortunately, we're hearing that a tree has fallen on the line up ahead. We're coming into Birch Valley, which will be our final stop.'

From near the front of the carriage came a cackle of laughter. 'Told you, didn't I?' came the old man's voice. 'Not seen snow like this since fifty-five.'

'I thought you said sixty-three, Grandad.'

'Nah, lad, talking 'bout one before that, ain't I? Snow so piled up we were trapped in there for weeks. Power out, only a wind up wireless for company. So cold we had to huddle together for warmth. Your old Grandpa was just eighteen years old that time. First time I ever went with a—'

'Dad!'

The old man chuckled. The young man in the window seat smiled as he stared at his newspaper. Across the aisle, the boy playing the game groaned, rolled his eyes, and began to tap faster and faster.

Birch Valley. Julia frowned. She didn't realise the train stopped there, because it was nothing more than a cluster of houses hidden among a few trees. Hardly even worth giving a name, but admittedly she couldn't remember ever going there. It was one of those places that you grow up knowing about, that's just up the road or just over the hill, but you never get around to visit because you don't know anyone who lives there, or its not on the road that you usually use. So even though it was no more than six miles from Olive Hill, she couldn't ever remember passing through. It had a church, maybe, she thought. Perhaps a small lake, or a river, being a valley after all. Wasn't there a tree farm?

She pulled out her phone to send a message to her parents, just to let them know. Perhaps they would be able to come out and pick her up, or the rail company would put on a bus to take any remaining passengers back to their hometowns. Three more stops after Birch Valley, but one glance out of the window and she knew she had a problem.

The snow was absolutely piling up. She could no longer see further than the edge of the rails where the light through the windows petered out, but it was piling up everywhere, drifting onto the tracks. They'd be lucky if they made it as far as Birch Valley. Perhaps they'd be stuck halfway there, buried in snow.

To her frustration, the snow was blocking her phone reception. She managed to send a quick message—*Mum, Dad, the train's delayed*—but her attempts to add some detail wouldn't send, and she began to get a no signal message whenever she tried.

The train began to slow down.

'Now arriving in Birch Valley,' the driver said through the speaker. 'All passengers please alight here. If Birch Valley is not your destination, please proceed to the waiting room next to the ticket office. We regret that it appears onward transportation will not be available until the snow clears. However, we are doing our best to arrange local accommodation for the night. In the meantime, please gather for some complimentary hot chocolate and marshmallows.' The children near the front of the carriage began to cheer. 'And we apologise again. However, on behalf of the station master, I'd like to welcome you to Birch Valley. Hopefully your stay will be short, but there's quite a storm going on, isn't there?'

2

ARRIVAL IN BIRCH VALLEY

THE TRAIN'S brakes gave a last tired squeal, followed by a hiss from further up the train and a little shudder as though the train itself was ready to take a break for the night. Julia copied the other passengers as they began to stand up and gather their belongings. To her disappointment, the young man with the newspaper had already headed to the doors between the two carriages, so perhaps he lived here in Birch Valley. She thought about surreptitiously following him, but the family with children had already bundled into the aisle and were getting their cases down from the luggage rail overhead. The boy opposite with the video game player had also got up and moved into the aisle, where he had decided to go through his rucksack, bent over with his back to Julia, leaving her with a less-than-pleasant view of his creased jeans bottom.

'All passengers alight here,' repeated the driver. 'Please go to the waiting room on the platform. If you're unsure where that is, look to the left when you get off the train, and look for the blue lettered sign. That's your one.'

Julia was last off the train, stepping over a pile of

snow that had accumulated along the platform edge. A grey-haired man who looked far too old for his station master's uniform was waving any passenger looking confused up the platform, a pair of orange gardening gloves that looked hastily found flecked with snowflakes. A couple of people tried to ask him about onward buses, but he just chuckled and nodded towards the ticket gates behind him where a few brave people were wading out into a snowy car park through snow drifts up to their knees.

'Good luck with that,' he said. 'Couldn't get a JCB through this.'

About twenty people had gathered inside the small waiting room, about double its natural capacity. An electric heater was cranked to maximum power, but to supplement it an old paraffin heater had been dragged into the centre, on the top of which stood a large vat of bubbling hot chocolate.

'Come on in and close the door,' said a ruddy-faced balding man in a dirty chef's hat. 'Keep what little heat there is inside. Right, we're about ready. Let's get you lot warmed up.'

Julia found herself squeezed into a corner between an old couple and a family with two young children. While the children seemed to be loving every moment of it—the boy tugging his father's jacket to demand they make a snowman *right now*, and the girl stuffing marshmallows into her mouth quicker than she could swallow them so that she resembled a squirrel but with longer hair—the parents appeared less so. The mother was frantically typing messages on her phone while the ashen-faced father nervously deflected his son's demands.

'Okay, that one sent,' the woman said. 'Mrs. Jenkins said she should be able to slip next door and put Danny out before he pees on the floor. Apparently it's not even snowing there. A few flakes, but mostly just slush.'

'I need to do a reading,' the old woman was saying, leaning against her husband's shoulder. 'I need to do one right now. This could be important. This could be the beginning of the apocalypse.'

'Can I grab a hot chocolate first?' the old man said. 'Not right to die without a decent drink in my hand. I see that guy's lacing the grown-ups' with brandy.'

'How can you think about alcohol at a moment like this?'

'Well, the apocalypse might be round the corner, but so is Christmas,' he said. 'One thing at a time, eh?'

'You're such an unbeliever.'

'I believe in Father Christmas.'

The woman sighed. 'Oh, Reginald. You're a lost cause.'

'Have you got one over there?' the mother of the family asked Julia. 'He's asking if you'd like it straight or with spice?'

'Excuse me?'

The woman gave a tired smile as though she'd asked the question a dozen times before. 'I think it must be local terminology. With or without brandy?'

'Oh … without, please,' Julia said. 'Although I wouldn't mind an extra marshmallow.' She smiled. 'Got to keep your strength up, haven't you?'

The woman chuckled as she took a paper cup of hot chocolate and passed it to Julia. 'That's right,' she said. 'Although I hope they'll figure something out soon. Quite unexpected, wasn't it?'

Julia nodded. 'The forecast said rain, didn't it?'

'Rain or sleet at worst. And what do we get? Two feet of snow.'

'Could be three or four by morning,' the husband said. 'I've never seen anything like it. Our part of Devon just turned into the Arctic.'

'It'll melt off quickly,' the woman said.

'And the flood will rise, and drown us all!' intoned the old woman from nearby, her hands raised towards the waiting room roof.

'Oh, Edwina, calm down,' Reginald said. 'Try some of this hot chocolate.'

'Are you from round here?' the woman asked Julia as Reginald took one of Edwina's hands and closed her fingers around a paper cup of hot chocolate. 'We're from Plymouth. There was supposed to be a bus from Olive Hill, but I don't think we're going to make it now. My name's Kelly, by the way. Kelly Wright. My husband is Colin, and the kids are Josh and Caitlin. We were only up in Brentwell for the pantomime matinee, since the Theatre Royal is closed for renovations this year. We thought it would be nice to take the train for a change.'

'It was a good thing you didn't drive,' Julia said. 'It would be a nightmare being stuck in this.'

'For sure. Are you a local?'

'Olive Hill. Two more stops and I was home. No idea how I'm going to get home now. I mean, it's six miles by road. On a nice day I might walk it, but not with my suitcase, and certainly not in this snow.'

'Best to sit tight, I think,' Kelly said. 'I mean, it wouldn't be nice having to hunker down in here for the night, but at least it's warm. And I'm sure that by tomorrow, the snow will have cleared and the trains will be running again.'

'You reckon?' Colin said, rubbing a circle in the mist on the window and peering out at the platform. 'It's still coming down. This room could end up our tomb if we're not careful. I wonder if they have an upstairs?'

'The apocalypse is upon us!' wailed Edwina, as Reginald patted her on the shoulder and offered embarrassed smiles to anyone who looked around.

'I recognise her from somewhere,' Kelly said. 'Isn't she on the telly?'

Colin leaned close. 'That's Edwina O'Fara. She's the breakfast time horoscopes woman on BestBetter TV.'

'BestBetter?'

Colin shrugged. 'It came free with our service but I cancelled it because it was rubbish. Josh was watching it one Saturday after you went to work, and she came on and made him cry.'

'Well, don't let him see her—'

'Mum!' Josh wailed suddenly, so predictably that even Julia could have foretold it. 'That's the scary woman off the telly! She said the whole village was going to fall into a pit of fire!'

'Quick, get him some hot chocolate!' Kelly hissed, as Colin steered Josh out of range. 'But no brandy!'

Luckily, Edwina, who had her eyes closed and was doing some kind of chant, hadn't appeared to notice. Reginald mouthed, 'Sorry!' in a way that suggested it was a common occurrence.

A sudden blown whistle cut off any further conversation, and everyone turned to look at the old station master standing in the waiting room doorway.

'Attention, please, ladies and gents,' he said. 'Me apologies for the snow. First we've had like this in thirty years or more so we're not really that prepared. Just spoke to one of the local farmers and he's going to come out with his digger and see if we can't at least clear the car park out there, but it could be a while. Luckily, we've got a few locals who've agreed to help until you can be on your way again.'

He opened the door and glanced up the platform, then called, 'Get a move on, lad!' A moment later, another old man in a duffel coat flecked with snowflakes and a Christmas hat pulled over his head came bundling into the room. The station master waved the assembled passengers back to make a little space, then stepped to the side to allow the newcomer some room. He took a moment to catch his breath, then straightened up and clapped his gloved hands with a dull thud.

'Well, ah, hello everyone,' he said. 'Everyone okay? No one hurt? No? Good, good. Did Stan here point you to the toilet?'

'Up platform, on left,' Stan said. 'Middle cubicle's blocked in the ladies, left cubicle in the mens.'

'Yes, that's right,' muttered the nervous man. 'Make sure not to use those.'

'Excuse me, but who exactly are you?' came a voice from the back of the group. 'If you're from the rail company, you've got some explaining to do.'

'No, no, I'm the chairman of Birch Valley Parish Council,' the man said. 'My name is Harry Faulkner. I'm afraid I wasn't expecting this situation, but the roads are blocked so badly not even the police can get through.'

'Figured a busybody like you'd be all over a mess like this,' Stan said, chuckling to himself.

'I'm not—'

'Anyone drops a sweet wrapper or forgets to bag a dog turd, you're dragging out the stocks,' Stan said, continuing to chuckle, before swigging out of a cup of hot chocolate.

'I think he's laced his a little too much,' Kelly whispered to Julia.

'Are you going to deal with this or waste our time?'

shouted the same man as before. Julia glanced over her shoulder and caught sight of a tall, dark-haired man in his fifties who looked like a policeman or a school headmaster.

'Yes, yes,' Harry stammered. 'Well, firstly, I'd like to welcome you to Birch Valley. We've always been a rather forgotten and secretive little community along the Brentwell Line, but there are many hidden delights to discover—'

'I need the toilet,' Josh whined to Kelly, as the man at the back shouted, 'Could you at least tell us how to get to the pub?'

Harry's hat fell off as he rubbed at his forehead, nearly landing on the stove burner, its course altered only by a desperate swipe of his hand. Instead, it landed on top of a pet carrier at the feet of an old woman. A brown and black striped paw darted out of a hole and made a swipe for the hat's pompom as it dangled over the side.

'Yes, yes, well, if you'd let me finish—'

'You haven't started yet!'

Colin rolled his eyes. 'Can you give it a rest back there?' he shouted at the tall man.

'Just trying to get some answers out of this fool.'

'If you zip it for five minutes he'll have a chance to.'

The man fell silent. Kelly grabbed Colin's arm and grinned at Julia. 'What did I do to deserve such a hero?' she said. 'Are you married?'

Julia forced a smile. It had been a while since she had last had a boyfriend, but the most recent two had been memorable. Dave, who she'd met online and dated for six months, had gone home with one of Julia's male work colleagues after a night at a club, while Tony, a man she had met in the local launderette after her washing machine had broken down, had stolen her car before later being arrested and charged with dealing stolen vehicles. He was currently serving a six-month prison sentence.

'I'm afraid not,' she said. 'I'm … ah, between boyfriends.'

'Right, well, let me explain what we've managed to do,' Harry said, staring at the hot chocolate in the bowl on top of the stove as though it was the only thing that could save him. 'I've rung around a few local residents, and we're in the process of arranging you all local accommodation for the next few days—'

'What do you mean, next few days?' the man at the back shouted.

'I'm going to lamp him in a minute,' Colin said, rolling his eyes at Kelly and Julia.

'I'm afraid, we're in a bit of a situation here—'

'The apocalypse!' wailed Edwina O'Fara.

'Mum, I'm going to wet myself!' Josh whined.

A sudden shrill whistle made everyone fall silent. Stan chuckled as he took it from his mouth and tucked it back into a breast pocket. 'Always wanted to do that,' he said. 'Now, the lot of you, shut up and let this man talk.'

'Right, so, we can't stay here,' Harry said, wiping a hand across his face which came away glistening with sweat. 'The pub is about a five minute walk up the street, so if you can manage it, we're going to reconvene there. I'm afraid we'll have to get through this snow, however, my wife, Barbara, is currently stringing up some lights to show you the way, it being dark and a little snowy and all. We're not sure how long you're all going to be stuck here, because all the phone lines have gone down. However, we're confident we can get the roads cleared in the next two or three days.' He clapped his hands together and grinned. 'You should all be home for Christmas. But … just in case you're not, we're putting together a few ideas to make a Birch Valley Christmas something you'll never forget.'

Caitlin cheered. After a moment of silence, everyone began to clap.

'Okay, now that's sorted, let's get everyone over to the pub for a welcome drink and a bit of orientation.'

As Harry headed back out on to the platform, waving at everyone to follow, Kelly leaned close to Julia.

'Quite exciting, isn't it? Like going on an adventure.'

Julia could only smile. It wasn't exactly what she had planned for the evening, but things were starting to look up.

ARRIVAL OF THE SNOW QUEEN

'Wow, look at that!'

'That's amazing!'

As the group emerged from the station's main entrance into a turning circle now two feet deep in snow, Julia was able to see what had got the children excited. In the centre of the turning area, a Christmas tree had been set up, but it was now completely covered in snow. The lights, however, continued to flicker and blink, illuminating what was little more than a ten-foot-tall white snow cone in red, yellow, and blue. In addition, someone had strung a line of fairy lights up the road, and they flickered out of the snowy gloom, leading up to a two-storey building on the corner with lights glowing with welcome through its downstairs window.

'That's the Deer and Grape,' Harry said. 'Follow the lights up the street, and please don't wander off. Donald, the landlord, promised there would be mince pies and Christmas cake waiting.'

As she followed Kelly's family through the snow, Julia tried to get a grip of her surroundings. Even though she had to have passed through Birch Valley a thousand times during train journeys to and from Brentwell, she couldn't ever remember having gotten off here. There was a main road a few miles to the east which completely bypassed it, and there were no specialist businesses or other reasons to visit. She had gone to primary school in Willow River, and remembered there was a school bus that had gone out here, but there had never been many kids on it. She wracked her brain, trying to remember names and faces, but all she could come up with was one weird kid called Danny who had once brought a mouse to school that he had allegedly found at the bus stop and put it into the teacher's desk drawer, and a girl called Verity who had stolen one of her hair clips and never given it back.

'Hey,' said a voice at her shoulder, and she turned to see the young man from the train walking beside her. 'Quite the turn in the weather, isn't it?'

Up close he looked older than he had from a distance, around Julia's age. He held a small suitcase in one hand and an umbrella in the other. Fat snowflakes pattered against it, then slid off on to the road.

Caught unawares, Julia opened her mouth to reply, only to catch her foot on something under the snow and stumble forward. She stuck out her only free hand, but it wasn't enough to stop her from crashing down into the snow. In a moment she was covered with the cold, wet stuff. She stood up, brushing herself down as the man held his umbrella over her. She couldn't bring herself to look at him as her hands ached with cold, her cheeks simultaneously burning with embarrassment.

'Oh, probably a rock or something,' he said, as she brushed snow off her suitcase, as even more slid off his umbrella and landed on top. 'Sorry about that. My name's Joseph. As in, Mary and.'

'Look, sorry, but it's a soft case, and I don't want to get it wet.'

'There'll be somewhere to dry it in the pub—'

'I don't really think you're helping, but thanks anyway—'

'Sorry.'

And he was gone, moving back along the line to help the old woman carrying the pet carrier with the cat inside, holding the umbrella over her head while she patted his arm and thanked him. They passed Julia as she was still standing by the side of the road, batting the relentless snowfall off her clothes and bag. She watched Joseph's back as he steered the old woman towards the welcoming lights of the pub, wondering if perhaps she hadn't been too harsh, then at the same time forgiving herself a little considering the conditions. After all, as she looked around, it seemed everyone was with someone else—if you counted the cat lady and her pet—except for her. As Edwina O'Fara, still muttering about the apocalypse, passed by with Reginald trying to both soothe her and downplay any likelihood that the world was set to end, Julia sighed.

She hadn't dressed for extreme weather, so by the time she reached the pub she was freezing cold, wet through, and covered from head to foot in snow, but as she walked through the door to join the rest of the stranded passengers, she couldn't help but smile. The pub was decked out for Christmas with a large, real tree in one corner, and fairy lights strung up all around the room and across the bar. The landlord looked like the resident Father Christmas lookalike with a large, grey-white beard hanging over a barrel-shaped chest, and even with a Christmas hat perched on his balding head.

'Welcome, welcome,' he called as people pushed

through the door. 'Drinks on the house. Get yourself settled down and dried off.'

A log fire was roaring in one corner. The old woman had let the cat out of his carrier, and he had quickly taken up residence on a chair near the fire. Kelly's kids had joined a couple of others for an impromptu game of pool. Edwina O'Fara was standing in one corner, chanting as she leaned her head against the wall, Reginald standing nervously nearby.

'You drink sherry?' Kelly asked, thrusting a glass towards Julia. 'It's good stuff.'

'Sure.'

The sharp liquid warmed her throat. Julia drank it a little quicker than she had intended, feeling it burn. She quickly began to feel better, however, when she looked around, she saw no sign anywhere of Joseph.

'Free drinks and a fire,' Kelly said. 'I suppose it could be worse. Do you think we'll all have to bed down in here?' She grinned at Colin. 'Husband here is quite a snorer.'

'No, I'm not!'

'How would you know? You're always asleep. It's me that has to suffer!'

'Don't listen to her,' Colin said. 'It's all lies.'

'Hey,' came an older man's voice. The noisy man from the waiting room patted Colin on the shoulder. 'I apologise for back there. A bit of a shock all round, isn't it?'

'Quite alright,' Colin said.

'My name's Jim. You look like a golfer. You play?'

'Handicap of nine.'

'Really? I'm at twelve. Been trying to knock another shot or two off for years. Can I get you a pint?'

'I don't think we're going anywhere soon, so sure.'

The two men turned away towards the bar, already lost

in conversation. Kelly shrugged. 'Looks like he's found a friend. Shall we get another drink too?'

Julia shrugged. 'I suppose so. Do you think we'll be able to get home in the morning? I'm supposed to be going back to my parents' for Christmas.'

Kelly laughed. 'I'm sure it'll be melted off by morning—'

The door opened with a sudden bang, and Harry Faulkner from the parish council, again flanked by Stan the station master, walked through. 'Donald,' he said, nodding curtly to the landlord.

'Harold,' Don replied.

'Look at them,' Kelly hissed into Julia's ear. 'They're totally brothers.'

'Hard to tell with the beard.'

'They are!'

'Ah, listen up, everyone,' Harry said, clapping his hands together. 'More bad news, I'm afraid. It looks like the snow's going to continue through tomorrow, meaning there's no chance any of you will be able to go home, unless you're crazy enough to try walking in this. However, we have managed to arrange enough local accommodation for all of you, so you'll all have a bed for the next couple of nights.'

'Goody goody,' Kelly said. 'I hope it's not in a hayloft—'

'Lord Andrews up at Birch Valley Grange has offered four rooms,' Harry said, to gasps from some of the passengers and a tut and a roll of the eyes from Don. 'Martin Smith at Clayfield Farm has two more, and the rest of you will be split among a handful of other local residences.'

Almost before he had stopped speaking, people began

putting their hands up, most demanding that they stay at the Grange.

'It could be haunted,' Kelly said. 'I mean, most old houses are, aren't they?'

Julia said nothing. It was like something out of a fairy tale, and she knew without even needing to know for sure that she would be chosen to stay at the Grange with this lord person. He was probably looking for a wife, and within a few days he would be down on one knee, asking for her hand in marriage. Wasn't that how it was supposed to be?

'Ah, please be quiet a moment,' Harry said, his voice all but lost in the cacophony until Don cracked a metal ladle down on the bar top.

'Quiet!' he hollered, then ran the ladle along the back of a line of hanging glass mugs, the sound almost musical.

The room fell quiet once again.

'Could any single people please raise their hands?'

It was almost as bad as being asked to wear a dunce hat. Julia tried to force her arm to rise, but it stayed where it was by her side.

'I don't literally mean single, but single here tonight,' Harry said. 'The rooms come in a variety of sizes, and it would make sense to allocate the largest to family groups.'

'That'll be you, then,' Kelly said, leaving Julia no choice but to tentatively raise her hand.

'Okay, the lady over there, and that gentleman, and—'

The door flew open, bringing with it a swirl of wind and snow. A woman dressed head to toe in white— presumably fake—fur stepped into the room. She could not have looked more ridiculous if a polar bear head had lolled off her shoulder, but in a white bobble hat and with cheeks that glowed like little red cherries, she was undeniably beautiful.

'Who ordered the snow queen?' Colin said.

'Stop staring at her,' Kelly scolded.

'She couldn't hold a candle to you, my love.'

'No, but maybe a fiery beacon.'

As the woman lifted a delicately gloved hand and said, 'I, regretfully, am currently single, although it is a status I don't intend to prolong,' Julia frowned, sure she had seen the woman somewhere before.

'Mum,' Caitlin said. 'That's *her*. That's the woman who rides the unicorn on TikTok!'

'It's a horse with a plastic horn taped to its head,' Colin said rolling his eyes.

'No, it's not. It's *real*.'

'What on earth would she be doing here?' Kelly said.

As though she had the ears of a hawk as well as the riding skills of a fairytale princess, the woman said, 'I'm afraid my limo will need digging out in the morning. I trust there are some strong, able gentlemen around here willing to help me?'

A couple of old men sitting at the bar raised their hands. 'Don't you say a word,' Kelly said to Colin.

Julia nearly clicked her fingers. That was it; she remembered now. Elizabeth Trevellian. She was a notorious media influencer, the type of person with a billion social media followers who actually did nothing practical in the real world. Julia was sure she'd read something about her being disgraced a year or two back, but she had obviously built herself back up again since.

'Alright,' Harry was saying. 'In that case, we'll put the gentleman over there into Clayfield Farm with Mr. and Mrs. O'Fara over there. And you, young lady,' he added, nodding at Julia, 'you can go with this intriguing lass in the white to Chapel Cottage, home of Joseph Swann and his delightful grandmother, Mabel.'

It took a moment for what had just happened to sink in. Julia was dimly aware of Kelly's family celebrating being allocated a room at the Grange and Elizabeth Trevellian proclaiming, 'I'll take the master bedroom, of course,' and then Joseph, he of the umbrella, was stepping forward out of the crowd, and giving Julia a shy, and somewhat awkward smile.

'But don't worry, everyone,' Harry said. 'I'm sure the roads will be dug out before you know it, and you'll all be on your way.'

4

DINNER AT CHAPEL COTTAGE

ELIZABETH TREVELLIAN, it turned out, came with an entourage. Standing outside the pub were two men. One looked barely out of school, a baseball cap holding down a ponytail as he fiddled with an expensive camera with gloved hands, while beside him was a tall man with close-cropped greying hair, an expensive suit, and sunglasses, one hand holding a phone to his ear while the other cupped an earpiece in his other ear.

'I think he's calling for backup,' Joseph quipped as he came up beside Julia.

'Oh, hi,' Julia said, feeling her cheeks flush. 'I'm sorry about earlier. I was a little sharp. I just want to go home, that's all.'

'I can understand. Where are you from?'

'My family live in Olive Hill, but I live up in Brentwell.'

'Oh? What do you do up there?'

'Ah … just office work. Insurance.'

'Sounds … interesting.'

'It's not. But it pays the rent. And you?'

'Excuse me,' Elizabeth said, waving a hand in front of

them as though to shoo their conversation away. 'I'm over here.'

'Hello,' Joseph said.

'We're freezing. Can you take us to our lodgings, please?'

'Ah, yes, certainly. Right, well, follow me.'

With an apologetic glance at Julia, Joseph headed off up the snowy street, wading through the snow, following a line of prints already made by a group that had recently gone that way. Julia started to follow, but the tall man stepped in front of her and put out his arms.

'Just a moment, please,' he said, as Elizabeth went first, following Joseph up the street, the young photographer trailing in her wake, his camera already in action as he attempted to get shots of the internet star from a multitude of directions.

Julia, wondering if perhaps she had fallen asleep on the train and was now in the middle of a bizarre dream, just shrugged, letting the situation take her along. After a moment, the man stepped back, bowed his head, and waved her forward.

'You may now proceed. Be careful of her dress. It cost as much as the car, and you don't want to start her moaning about it, believe me.'

Certain the man was making some kind of joke, Julia glanced over at him, and found a small smile on his lips. Behind the sunglasses, his eyes were unreadable.

'Quite some snow, isn't it?' she said, attempting to make conversation.

'For this mild little country,' he said in a deep, thunderous voice that made Julia think of a train bumping over sleepers.

'You're not … from round here?'

The man shook his head. 'Norway.'

'Oh. Well, my name's Julia. Julia Adams. Some people call me Julie, but whichever you remember.'

'Magnus,' the big man said. 'Magnus Sorensen. I'm Ms. Trevellian's driver. I also double as the security.'

'Does she need much of it in a place like Birch Valley?'

A smile crept on to Magnus's face again. 'No. But let's not tell her. I remain hopeful of a Christmas bonus.'

They were coming up to a junction where a single street light illuminated a sheet of falling snow. The snowy outline of a farm gate was the only thing to break the white mounds of buried hedgerows. As Joseph waved for them to turn left, Elizabeth stopped and turned back, flapping a hand at Magnus.

'Magnus! Can you have a quick check in there for any hiding paps?'

Magnus's face remained as stoic as ever, but standing close to him, Julia heard a deflating breath come from his mouth.

'Yes, Ms. Trevellian,' he answered. 'Carry on after the young man and I'll have a look for you. There is a strong possibility there could be some paparazzi hiding in that field, despite the absence of any tracks or other disturbance.'

'You are a dear.'

As Elizabeth headed on after Joseph, Magnus inclined his head slightly, his brow furrowed. 'If the paparazzi are hiding in the field, I'm sure they are frozen by now, like the ice statue.'

Chapel Cottage was set back from the road down a narrow driveway, right where the road made a right-angled turn and rose uphill for five yards or so to a small car park outside the chapel that had given the cottage its name. The snow had eased a little, but it was still dark, and both the cottage and the chapel up the road were illuminated only by a single light outside each, leaving the road between a dark, snowy smudge, its details to be filled in. The cottage, though, stonewalled and with overhanging eaves that protected rows of plant pots from being buried, was like something out of a postcard. Even though her feet and most of her body were soaked, Julia couldn't help but smile as they trudged up the driveway.

They were almost there when the front door opened and a diminutive woman in a floral apron stepped outside, accompanied by the distinct aroma of freshly baked mince pies.

'Welcome to Chapel Cottage,' she said. 'How many have we got?'

Joseph turned and waved the others forward. 'Well, there's the two ladies, Julia and Elizabeth,'—it wasn't lost on Julia that he said her name first, and she turned away to hide a smug smile even as Elizabeth scowled, '—and the two guys, ah—'

'Magnus,' Magnus said.

'And this is X,' Elizabeth said, pointing to the photographer, who was currently squatting on the snow, attempting to photograph Elizabeth against the backdrop of the cottage eaves.

'X?'

'Just X,' Elizabeth said. 'It's a digital calling card. X has gone beyond names.'

Mabel exchanged a glance with Joseph, who shrugged. 'Right … well, I've made up the spare rooms for the two ladies, and put down a camp bed in Joseph's room for Magnus. And ah, X, you can take the sofa bed in the living room.'

'X doesn't sleep,' Elizabeth said. 'He meditates on existence.'

'How intriguing,' Mabel said. 'I assume he hasn't gone beyond food? Because I've prepared a little something. If you'll all follow me through to the dining room, we'll get you dried off and warmed up.'

They all took off their shoes in the entrance, leaving them on a sheet of newspaper Joseph had laid out. Magnus took up a position by the front door—still with his sunglasses on—but Mabel shook her head.

'What on earth are you doing?'

'My duty,' Magnus said, presumably staring straight ahead, although how he could see anything with sunglasses on, Julia wasn't sure. 'How many of the entrance and the exit are there?'

'Well, there's the back door....'

'Aerial? Or under the ground?'

'There's a skylight in the loft, but the hinges are a bit rusty. It hasn't opened in years—'

'And I need to check your phones. No photos or videos will be taken during our stay.'

Elizabeth was standing nearby, her arms folded, a look of pride on her face. Julia standing barefoot having removed her socks, just shook her head. She wanted to say something, but everything felt too surreal, and nothing she could think of seemed appropriate ... so she stayed quiet.

'I think we all need to calm down a little bit,' Joseph said. 'I think it's pretty clear that no one can get into or out of the village right now—'

'My worry is not the people,' Magnus said. 'It's the digital. Drones, bots ... spy software.'

Mabel stamped her foot on the ground. 'I've made mince pies,' she said. 'And they're getting cold. Now, you can go in there and eat them, or you can head off down to the village and sleep under a tree. Do I make myself clear?'

Joseph was staring at his grandmother with a sparkle of pride in his eyes. X was fiddling with his camera. Magnus looked at Elizabeth.

'Does she make herself clear?'

Elizabeth frowned for a moment, then rubbed a chin that looked surgically contoured. 'Yes, I believe she does. You may stand down for the evening.'

'Thank you.'

Magnus reached up and took off his sunglasses, revealing sparkling green eyes. Then, he loosened his tie a little, and rubbed his hands together.

'So … you made the mince pies?'

Mabel smiled. 'As many as you can eat. And don't worry about protecting the princess here, we've got Basil, in case there's any trouble.'

'I'm not a princess, I'm an influencer—'

'Basil?'

Mabel clapped her hands together. 'Come here, boy.'

Julia gasped as a monstrous shadow fell across the wall from a side room, followed by a massive grey-brown shaggy thing she assumed was a dog, although beneath the hair it could easily have been a small bear. He came easily up to Julia's waist and possibly outweighed her. As she stood frozen against the wall in fear, he lumbered up to her, gave her hand a sniff, then went from person to person, investigating each in turn. Elizabeth looked horrified, while X dropped into a manicured stance and took a photo. The dog seemed to settle on Magnus, licking his hand, then sitting down at his feet and staring at him, tongue lolling.

'He's an otterhound,' Mabel said. 'Only about six hundred left in the world.'

'His feet have the webs,' Magnus said, squatting down

to pat the dog on the head. 'It makes him swim strong, and makes him buoyant in the snow.'

'You know dogs well,' Mabel said.

'My mother bred St. Bernards. In the northern fjords, there is much need for dogs used to snow.'

'I think Basil can tell. He always knows a dog person when he sees one.'

After a little more fussing over the dog, during which at one point X lay on the ground to take an action shot, only for Basil to climb on top of him and lie down, tongue dripping all over the photographer's face, they made it to the dining room, where Mabel had set out a mouth-watering selection of sandwiches, cakes, sausage rolls, and of course, mince pies.

With the conversation stunted and awkward, Julia concentrated on the food, stuffing herself until she thought she might burst. Joseph sat at one end of the table with Magnus at the other. Julia sat on one side alongside Elizabeth, with Mabel and X on the other. Elizabeth, she noted, ate only the lettuce and cucumber slices from inside a few sandwiches, handing the bread to Magnus, who hoovered down anything within range. Julia noted with a smile that while X might have moved beyond names, he had no such qualms about food, and for a while went toe to toe with Magnus on the mince pies.

'So, what is it you do?' Mabel asked, after the pace of eating had begun to slow a little. With the reflection of the overhead light on Mabel's spectacles making it unclear to whom she was speaking, Julia opened her mouth to answer, only for Elizabeth to lean forward and say, 'I'm an influencer.'

'That's nice, dear. What do you influence?'

'People.'

'Oh, really. So, like a politician then?' She glanced at

Joseph, giving him a sly smile. 'What a bunch of devious snakes they are.'

'No, not like a politician at all,' Elizabeth said. 'I influence people on lifestyle. What to wear, how to behave, what to listen to, for example.'

'How is that different to a politician?'

Elizabeth looked stumped. She glanced at Magnus for support, but the big security guard was delicately cutting a sausage roll into neat slices.

'Ah—'

'So what brings you to our little part of the country?'

'We heard about the snow and thought it would be a good opportunity for a photo shoot. Something winter-themed.'

'You don't take holidays, then?'

Elizabeth sighed. 'It's the algos. If you lose the algos, your popularity can plummet.'

'What's an "algo"? Is that some relation to the stuff you find in ponds?'

'Algorithm,' Elizabeth said with a heavy sigh. 'It's how internet sites define your popularity. Of course, having millions of supporters helps, but you're either growing or you're shrinking, aren't you?'

'I'm pretty sure I'm just shrinking, aren't I, Joseph?'

'You've got a few years left yet, Granny,' Joseph said, helping himself to another mince pie.

'You people with your simple lives just don't understand,' Elizabeth said, rolling her eyes. 'Content, content, content. If you can't produce more content … All. The. Time … you'll swiftly become a nobody. She lifted an arm. These Versace handwoven sweaters won't buy themselves, you know.'

'They do a great imitation in Primark up in Exeter,' Mabel said. 'Joseph got me one for Christmas last year.'

Elizabeth gave a dramatic sigh. 'I'll turn in now,' she said.

There was a flurry of activity as X and Magnus moved to assist Elizabeth. Mabel bade them follow her, and together they headed out of the room, leaving Julia and Joseph alone. Perhaps attracted by the sudden quiet, Basil padded back in from the hall and laid his head over Joseph's lap. Joseph leaned forward to peer through the open doorway, then slipped the dog a sly sausage roll, which disappeared in a few seconds.

'Thank you for taking me in,' Julia said, finally finding the courage to speak. 'I really appreciate it.'

'No problem at all,' Joseph said. 'I'm sorry it's not a little more peaceful.'

Julia smiled. 'My sister has four children. If I'd made it to my parents' house, it would have made this look like a poker game.'

'You don't have any children?'

Caught off guard, Julia shook her head. 'No … not yet. I mean, I've never been with anyone long enough to start thinking about it.'

Joseph nodded. 'Me neither.' He looked about to say something else, but then rubbed his hands together and stood up. 'I suppose I should start putting this all away—'

Basil's head lifted, the big dog peering towards the window. One ear pricked up. A moment later the faint sound of a distant howl came from somewhere outside.

Julia shivered. 'Was that what I think it was?'

Joseph grimaced. 'A wolf. Yeah.'

'There are wolves around here? This is England; I didn't think there were any.'

'Only three. Currently. We're expecting a few more in the coming days, actually.'

Joseph pushed Basil away and stood up as the howl came again. 'I'm afraid I have to go,' he said.

'Outside?'

'Yeah.'

'Right now?'

'Right now. That howl … that's Barry. He's our resident male. He's howling because the snow must have broken the fence.'

'You have a *wolf*?'

'Ah … yeah. And it sounds like he just got out.'

5

WOLF ON THE HUNT

BASIL LOOKED KEEN for a walk in the snow, but Joseph called down the hallway to Mabel and then shut the big dog in a side room beside the kitchen. Julia watched Joseph as he pulled a dog lead out of a kitchen cupboard and then found a hat in a box beside the back door.

'I'll come with you,' she said, standing up.

'It's not a good idea.'

'You're holding a lead. This wolf of yours can't be that dangerous.'

'Only to local sheep. Look, if you promise to stay close. The snow's really bad out there.'

'I noticed.'

'Okay, give me a minute. You can't go out dressed like that, and your jacket's soaked.'

'Do you have something I can borrow?'

It took a couple of minutes of rummaging through a cupboard, but soon Julia was kitted out with a thick winter jacket, hat, gloves, fresh woolly socks, and a pair of spare boots that apparently were Joseph's old pair. It alarmed her slightly that they had the same sized feet, even that the boots were a little tight. Joseph didn't give her time to worry much about it, though, as he handed her a torch and said, 'Are you ready? I mean it, stay close, and do what I say.'

'Got it. Is this wolf of yours likely to attack me?'

Joseph shrugged. 'No … well, he might. I mean, he is a wolf.'

'Is he more dangerous than Basil?'

'On a scale of one to ten, with Basil as a five?'

'Well, I suppose—'

Before Joseph could complete his answer, the howl came again, closer this time.

'You don't have to come. The snow's still coming down, and it could be dangerous.'

Julia glanced over her shoulder. Down the corridor, Elizabeth was complaining about the strength of the coat hangers and the depth of the bedroom's wardrobe.

'I'll come,' she said.

Joseph took the lead with Julia following along behind. The snow had eased a little, but with the flakes reflecting the glare of the torches it was hard to see more than a few metres ahead.

At first they followed a farm lane that ran downhill behind the house, before finding themselves surrounded by trees. Rather than towering over their heads, though, most of the trees barely reached above head height, providing them no cover at all. And strangely, many of them appeared to be glowing, illuminating the snow that covered their branches with colourful lights.

'What's that coming from?' Julia asked, waving her torch at the trees.

'That's our farm,' Joseph said. 'We—look! Tracks! Ah, it looks like he's gone up to the hilltop. Typical wolf. He's looking for a moon to howl at. Good luck with that tonight.'

The land began to incline upwards. The lines of regular trees topped with lights gave way to natural forest, the trees larger, their branches laden with snow, leaving the ground clearer and easier to traverse. Joseph seemed to be following a rough path up through the forest, his torch beam illuminating a line of tracks to the right that moved haphazardly from tree to tree as they headed uphill, as though the wolf had been marking his territory as he went.

Julia hadn't spent much time in the great outdoors over the last few years, and found herself out of breath. Joseph, clearly accustomed to such arduous climbing, had to pause several times to let her catch up.

'I'm sorry,' she gasped, as she climbed up through the snow to a clearing where he waited. 'I should have let you go alone. I'm not used to this.'

'It's okay,' he said. 'It's nice to have some company. I think the sky has cleared. We might get a good view from the lookout point at the top, if we're lucky. I imagine that's where we'll find Barry, too.'

Julia wasn't sure what to expect from the supposed view, but five minutes of climbing later the trees parted around them, and she found herself on a bald, snow-covered hilltop which offered a panoramic view of the surrounding area. A full moon shone overhead, and the snow that covered everything for as far as they could see reflected its glow, giving the whole world a surreal, dreamlike feel. The lights of villages spotted distant valleys like speckles of fairy glitter, and a clear line through the surrounding fields indicated the railway as it passed through Birch Valley and on towards Olive Hill.

'Ha, there he is,' Joseph said.

He lifted his torch for a moment, but it wasn't

necessary. A shape had jumped up on to a snow-laden picnic bench on the very top of the hill, and as Julia watched, it sat back on its haunches, lifted its head to the sky, and let out a long, haunting howl. A tingle ran down her spine, and perhaps for the first time since getting off the train, Julia was pleased that circumstances had worked out as they had.

'He's such a show-off,' Joseph said. Then, clicking his fingers, he called, 'Barry, come here.'

The wolf leapt down off the table. Julia lifted her torch and her breath caught in her throat. The wolf was bounding towards them, tongue lolling, the torchlight glinting off his teeth. This was a wolf, she reminded herself, the awe she had felt moments before replaced by fear. She started to step back behind Joseph, only for him to squat down, opening his arms.

'Come on, do the jump thing,' he called, and Barry obliged, leaping the last few feet to land in Joseph's arms. While not as big as Basil, he was large enough to knock Joseph back into Julia, who found herself lying on her back. A silhouette rose over her, and she gasped, the breath caught in her throat.

'No—'

A thick, wet tongue slapped the side of her face, then a heavy panting creature sat down on top of her, paws resting on her chest.

'He's caught you,' Joseph said, clipping a collar and lead around the wolf's neck. 'Look how proud he is.' He rubbed the wolf's neck. 'Look at you,' he said. 'You're a proper wolf now, aren't you? Howling at the moon, catching a human. What are we going to do with you?'

'Any chance you could move him?' Julia gasped.

'Oh, sorry! Come on, Barry. Up you get. Let her free.'

He pulled the wolf away, then reached down and

helped Julia up. She climbed to her feet, brushing snow off her clothes.

'Are you alright?'

'I'm fine,' Julia said, aware her voice was becoming alarmingly high. 'I don't think I've ever had a wolf sit on me before. It's quite a … novel experience.'

Joseph pointed the torch down at the wolf now sitting at his feet. 'Don't tell him, but he's only part wolf. His mother was a Siberian Husky. He'd be heartbroken if he knew.'

'Can I ask why you even own a wolf?'

'It was my grandmother's thing,' he said. 'She's been keeping them for years. She trains them and then rents them out for film work. Barry here has starred in roughly a dozen different films over the last five years.'

'Oh my god, really?'

'Yes. Although work is drying up. Most films these days use stock footage or CGI. It's not very exciting. They film him running about in front of a green screen for a couple of days, then they edit the footage into their projects.'

'That's still pretty cool.'

'He's mostly just the star attraction of our little farm petting zoo. Well, at least until the pups are born.'

'How exciting. I had no idea there was anything like this going on in Birch Valley.'

'Most people tend to blink and miss it as they pass through on the train, but they miss a lot.' He started forward. 'Come on, let's go and have a look at the view before we go back down.'

They walked to the hilltop, where Joseph cleared the snow away from what was indeed a picnic table. The snow was so deep that they had to sit on the top with their feet on the seats. Tied to one of the legs, Barry wandered about in the snow nearby.

'It looks how I imagined Norway or Canada might look,' Julia said, shaking her head. 'It's … beautiful.'

'Can I show you something else?'

'Sure.'

They climbed down from the table. Joseph untied Barry and they headed back the way they had come, but instead of taking the footpath down into the woods, Joseph took another one that headed to a second, slightly lower lookout point on the eastern side of the hill. Here, the surrounding hills were closer, blocking their view of the distant countryside, but as the valley below opened out, Julia gasped.

Everywhere, thousands upon thousands of lights twinkled in the branches of hundreds of trees.

'I saw some on the way up, but I didn't realise … it's so pretty. Wow.'

'That's my family's farm,' Joseph said. 'We farm Christmas trees.'

'They come with lights?'

Joseph chuckled. 'No, that was kind of my pet project. They're solar powered. I thought it would be nice for people to see how their tree might look. It took forever to string them all. This is possibly a one-off experience, though. All the sensors are now buried, so they won't light up again until after the snow starts melting off.'

Julia took another step forward to peer further down the slope, and at that moment, her foot caught on something buried under the snow. As she stumbled, she stuck out a hand, reaching for whatever was closest. It turned out to be Joseph's wrist. She had dropped her torch at the same time, and it somehow landed beam upwards, illuminating them both. She hadn't really had time to study him before, but up close his green eyes were filled with kindness, he had a nice smile … and she could feel the strength in his arms. They didn't live so far apart, and they were about the same age. His eyes held on to hers as he helped her up, then the torch sank in the snow and he became a silhouette against the sky once more.

'Sorry,' she muttered, letting go of his arm. 'Thanks for … helping me.'

'It's alright,' he said, his voice sounding a little strained, as though it was suddenly hard to speak. 'We should … we should head back.'

They barely said anything as they followed the footpath back down the hill, through the trees, and along the road to the cottage. Joseph muttered about being careful a couple of times, and Julia grunted monosyllabic responses. As the lights of the cottage came in sight up ahead, Joseph stopped.

'Are you okay from here? I need to put Barry back into his enclosure. Much as I'd like to let him into the house, he tends to play with Basil, and the result is utter chaos.'

'Sure, I'll be fine.'

'See you later then?'

'Sure.'

As Julia headed back to the cottage alone, she wasn't sure whether she was walking on air or wading through mud. She had felt that little tingle as she looked at Joseph in the torchlight, that feeling that told her she was attracted, and now she just felt uncomfortable. Unless he was hiding a wife or girlfriend somewhere, he looked single, and so was she, even if it was only a few months since her last failed relationship had ended.

With seasonal familiarity, the doubts began to creep in. They were worse as she got older, she had found; once she wouldn't have cared about anything except what was in the minute, but now everything was about the future: was he interested enough, would it last, were they suited? Did she want to be with a man from the countryside who ran a Christmas tree farm, or should she hold out just that little longer?

She couldn't help it. Getting out of a bad relationship at thirty-five had left her more fragile than she liked to admit.

She went into the house, took off the boots and hung the coat up on a hook. The corridor was dark, but a thin glow beneath the door meant a light was still on in the kitchen, so she knocked lightly on the door, then opened it and peered inside.

Mabel was standing by the kitchen worktop. Beside her, impossibly large, stood Magnus, wearing a floral apron so small it looked more suited to a doll, the strings so stretched they'd used a clip to hold the ends together. On the other side of Mabel, X was standing with his camera, angling it down at the worktop.

'And you crimp it like this, but don't press too hard or the pastry will be too compacted. You want a nice, soft crimp so that the pastry bakes a little flaky.'

'Sorry to interrupt,' Julia said. 'We … ah … went out to find Barry.'

Mabel turned to her and smiled. 'Oh, he's a pesky one,' she said. 'He's out at the first opportunity, howling away at the moon. He thinks he's a proper wolf. Why don't you come and join us? The empress has turned in because apparently she needs fourteen hours of sleep per night, so we're having a bit of a cooking lesson. Have you ever made a mince pie?'

Julia shook her head. 'I've only ever bought them from a shop.'

'Well, now's your chance to learn. Grab an apron from that cupboard over there. Right, Magnus, it's your turn. Remember what I said about the crimping….'

6

BREAKFAST TIME

JULIA WOKE up with a heavy head, but both her grogginess and her mood cleared the moment she opened the curtains of her upper floor room to find a glorious snowy landscape waiting outside.

She had been allocated a small attic room with a sloping ceiling above the bed, but the end of the room was at the back of the house and looked out over snow-covered gardens, into a field beyond which stretched away to a patch of woodland, and then to the hill she guessed was the same one she had climbed last night with Joseph. With the snow covering everything, it was difficult to figure out what was what, but in the garden someone had dug a path through the snow to a raised patio and cleared the snow off a picnic table and a set of chairs.

She opened the window, letting in a chilly breeze. A bird called in the distance, the only sound over the dripping of water. She had to admit to feeling a little disappointed; typical England, it would probably be melted off by tomorrow and all gone by Christmas Day.

She checked her phone, relieved to find she now had a

couple of bars of reception. Her mother had sent a message—*Are you still on the train?*—just after midnight, and Julia felt a sudden pang of guilt for not responding. She called her mother, pressing the phone to her ear.

'Julia?'

The signal was dipping in and out, but Julia could just about make out her mother's voice on the other end of the line. 'It's me. Sorry, Mum. Yesterday was a bit of a nightmare but I'm fine. I'm in Birch Valley. The train got delayed here by the snow, but some locals put us up.'

'Oh, thank goodness. We did try calling the rail company. It was on the local news that everything was delayed, but hopefully it'll be cleared soon. You should be here for Christmas, shouldn't you?'

Julia checked the date on her phone, having felt disorientated since yesterday. December 19th.

'No problem. I might even be there later today.'

'Oh, I doubt that. The news said the snow on the line had drifted five feet high in places, but all the roads are blocked so nothing can get in to clear it. Apparently a couple of snow ploughs are driving down from Scotland, but they'll take a day or two to get here.'

Julia's heart sank. 'Maybe tomorrow then.'

'I'm sure you'll be here before you know it. One other thing I ought to mention—your father's cousin Albert's family showed up yesterday. You remember Albert, don't you?'

'Is that the one who changed his socks six times a day and left them lying everywhere?'

'Ah, you remember. Yes, well, he has a skin condition. Anyway, they showed up yesterday in their campervan. They were going down to Penzance for Christmas, but decided to stop over at ours until the snow cleared.

Unfortunately the campervan's heating system is broken so we've had to put them up in the house.'

Julia felt like she was standing outside in the snow, slowly sinking. Albert's family had only visited once that she remembered. They lived off the grid. Showers were anathema and all property was considered communal. Plus, they had set her hamster free, claiming cages were cruel. The family cat had brought it back later. What was left of it.

'So … they're at the house?'

'Yes, we've had to put Cassandra and Ebony in your room. Don't worry, we've got a camp bed for you out in the conservatory. Dad's put a heater in there so you'll be quite snug.'

'Okay … thanks.'

'So we'll see you tomorrow or the next day?'

Julia had a lump in her throat. 'Ah … yeah.'

She hoped the first train would be going straight back to Brentwell. A Christmas alone with Mittens was preferable to dealing with Dad's cousins. Her sister was with their parents; she could deal with everything, and Julia would do her bit by offering a telephone ear for the horror stories once Christmas was over.

'Well, you have a nice time in Birch Valley. I hope you've got some books to read. I remember the car broke down there once, back before they re-opened the train line. Your Dad and I almost died of boredom waiting for the breakdown lorry.'

'Okay, I'll try. See you soon, Mum.'

'Yes, and you love. Chin up!'

Julia hung up the call before she could start sobbing into the phone. So, Christmas was going to be rubbish. She was trapped in the middle of nowhere, and even if she could somehow escape, two banshees in human form had taken over her old room.

Perhaps it was for the best. She was thirty-five after all, and while her old bedroom had long since ceased to contain any of her things and had been reverted to guest room status, it had always been a given that when she visited it would be hers. Perhaps being relegated to the conservatory would do her good.

She went downstairs, hoping to find Mabel, or at worst, Joseph. From the living room downstairs, however, came a series of barks and yelps, not all of them from Basil. Julia cracked the living room door and peeked through.

'Grunt like you're lifting that bale,' snapped an angry woman's voice from the television. 'Come on, you three-legged pigs. That butter isn't going to churn itself.'

Mabel was lying on a yoga mat, wearing a tracksuit, trying to lift one leg off the floor. Elizabeth perched on the edge of a sofa nearby, and appeared to be offering encouragement. On the screen, an angry-looking woman with tattoos poking out from her gym gear was lying on her back in the middle of a barn while a handful of bored cows looked on from an enclosure nearby. She was making bicycle motions with her feet, then slapped a butter churn standing near her head.

'Churn! Churn, you worms! Are you hurting yet? If you're not hurting, you're not trying!'

Then, in a sudden jarring break of the fourth wall, she rolled over and sat up. 'That's all for today,' she said, glaring at the camera. 'See you tomorrow. And I'll know if you're not there. Trust me, I'll know.'

As she scowled into the camera, credits appeared on the screen, and a voiceover said, 'If you're enjoying Doreen's thirty-day farm workout, don't forget to subscribe.'

'I met Doreen once,' Elizabeth mused, as a sweaty, exhausted Mabel tried to roll over and get up. 'In person she's lovely. Prison really helped her. We did a double live once and had over a million views.'

Mabel was still struggling to get up. Julia steeled herself, then opened the door with a cheery 'Good morning!', and went straight to help Mabel up on to the nearest armchair.

'Oh, you're up,' Elizabeth said. 'Was that you snoring in the night? It seemed to come right down through the floor.'

Julia was still searching for words to respond when Mabel patted her on the knee, gave her a sly wink and then said to Elizabeth, 'Probably just the pipes. We can't afford to get those fixed either.'

Julia sensed she had entered into the middle of an ongoing conversation, but before she could bring herself to say anything, Elizabeth said, 'Well, I can offer you Magnus for the morning to chop some firewood, once he's checked the perimeter for drones, hiding paparazzi, and news helicopters. If that would help?'

Mabel smiled. 'It would save Joe doing it. He has fences to mend, by the sound of things.'

The door banged open and Basil came lumbering into the room. He gave Elizabeth a disinterested sniff, then made a beeline for Julia, putting his paws up on her knees, tongue lolling happily.

'Oh, could you hold that pose a moment? That would make a wonderful photograph. Don't worry, we'll blur your face or edit it out.'

'I … ah….'

Too late, Basil had jumped down and wandered over to Mabel. 'He's hungry,' the old woman said. 'I imagine you are too. Give me half an hour. Anyway, who wants to help me in the kitchen is most welcome.'

'Sure,' Julia said, at the same moment that Elizabeth said, 'I need to exfoliate.'

Julia followed Mabel into the kitchen while Elizabeth went back to her room. Mabel fed Basil, who gulped his food down in a few massive mouthfuls, then retired to a basket by the back door.

'I'm sorry if I interrupted anything,' Julia said.

Mabel chuckled. 'Oh no, dear. I like to do my ten minutes of exercise every day, even at my age. I don't have much flexibility these days, though. The other girl was just keeping me company.'

'You have a lovely place here. This cottage, and the surrounding area, it's just delightful.'

'It's been in my family for generations,' Mabel said with a sigh. 'I grew up in this house, and when my parents passed away, I took over the business. Times are changing, though, aren't they?'

Julia was clued up enough about the modern world to know what Mabel was talking about. 'You're closing?'

Mabel passed her a couple of bananas and a chopping knife, then opened the oven door, slid out a tray, and began to lay thick slices of bacon over the metal grill.

'We might not have a choice,' she said. 'We run a wildlife sanctuary and a tree farm. The last couple of years have been pretty tough. We used to get all the families during the holidays, but all kids do these days is stare at little screens and press buttons. No one's interested in otters or wild geese. And since that new garden centre opened on the Brentwell to Willow River road, tree sales have sunk. Our beautiful little pines can't compete with cheap and easy plastic.'

'I'm sorry to hear that.'

Mabel shrugged as she slid the grill back into the oven. 'That's life, I suppose. There's nothing much you can do about these things. You either take it on the chin and try to adapt, or you die.' She chuckled. 'And while Joseph might still have plenty of life in him, mine's running out.'

'Don't say that! I wouldn't put you at a day over … sixty-five?'

Mabel laughed as Julia smiled. 'I'm seventy-eight, but I appreciate it. Perhaps it's the country air, keeping me young.'

'For sure. It's lovely round here. I mean, I think it is. I can't really tell with all this snow.'

'Ah, don't worry, it'll melt in a day or two. This is England after all. I bet you're looking forward to getting home.'

'Well … I was, but then I heard from my mother that the cousins from hell have shown up, and the two demon daughters are sharing my old room. As soon as they open the train line up again, I'll probably just go back to Brentwell and celebrate with my cat in front of the telly. My neighbour's looking after her, so she's probably missing me.'

'Oh, dear, that's terrible. Why don't you just stay here? We've got plenty of room, and I'd love a bit of help while Joseph's out clearing the snow. Plus, there's a bit of a local celebration coming up, so you could stay for that.'

'I'm sorry, but I really couldn't impose. I mean, I only just met you yesterday, and while it's lovely of you to let me stay, I couldn't impose on you longer than I have to.'

'You're no trouble at all. Do you know, before his dear parents departed in that terrible accident, we used to run this place as a farm-themed B&B. We always had people here. In fact, that's where my dear son met his lovely wife —God rest their poor souls—and it's been so nice having a bit of noise in the house. Joseph, he's so quiet with his books and his writing, I sometimes feel like I'm living here alone. That snowstorm was a godsend for me—'—she leaned close, dropping her voice to a whisper—'—even if *she's* like something out of a glossy teen magazine. I said a little prayer to the sky yesterday to give us another dump of snow this afternoon, just to keep you all here.'

Ignoring the connotations of being kidnapped, however well meaning, Julia smiled. 'Well, I suppose we'll see.'

Mabel looked up at her and winked. 'Plus, I noticed Joseph looking at you yesterday.'

Julia's cheeks flushed. 'No, he was probably looking at Elizabeth.'

'She was on the other side of the table. I suppose he could have been looking at Magnus, but I'm pretty sure he's swimming on this side of the river, if you know what I mean.'

'Ah….'

'He's a good boy, is my grandson. A bit of a—what do you say?—an introvert? What with all his poetry and stuff. But he's got a kind heart.'

Julia was aware that she was sweating, and having not yet had a shower, probably looked awful with her bedhead and without any makeup.

'I'm … I'm sure he'll find the perfect someone sooner or later.'

Mabel pulled open the grill door and a puff of smoke wafted out. 'Oh dear,' she said with a chuckle. 'Might be a little on the blackened side. Still, a little carbon never hurt anyone. I suppose I could get Magnus to go out there and slaughter another pig. I bet he looks great in a vest—'

'It'll be fine,' Julia said quickly. 'Shall I call the others?'

'Yes, please dear. Tell them five minutes. I'll just get the toast started, and then we can talk about the plans for the day.'

7

HONOURED GUESTS

T HE PHONE RANG while they were at breakfast, Mabel rushing off to answer it. Joseph hadn't shown up—according to Mabel he was still out mending the fence of the wolf enclosure—so Julia sat on one side of the table next to Magnus, who looked capable of giving Basil a run for his money in the speed eating stakes. Three times he politely asked Julia to pass extra toast from a plate Mabel had knowingly loaded with far more than should have been necessary to feed a small army. Sitting opposite, Elizabeth, now immaculately dressed in a beige fur-trimmed sweater and black ski trousers, the clips in her hair probably more expensive than Julia's entire wardrobe, ate only a couple of leaves of lettuce and a sliced tomato. Beside her, X was a little more indulgent, making a bacon sandwich and stuffing a corner into his mouth, before catching Elizabeth's eye and proceeding to chop the rest of it up into neat triangles, which he arranged in a geometric pattern on his plate before eating them one by one in sequence, like a countdown timer.

'I think you should cover the vehicle with a tarpaulin,'

Elizabeth said between slices of tomato. 'Some of my competitors would have a field day if they knew what had happened. I can see it now—"Elizabeth Trevellian—ice statue or icicle?"'

X, head down, grinned, quickly hiding it. He looked up at Elizabeth, gave her a dismayed expression and shrugged.

'And what if Google Maps updates while we're stuck? You know they only do it every ten years or so? I could be run off everything as a laughing stock. My online career would be over. I'd have to go back to conventional magazines.'

She lowered her head, apparently sobbing. X patted her on the shoulder.

Magnus looked at Julia and smiled. Then, to Elizabeth, he said, 'There is no concern unless they now have the treads of a caterpillar.'

'They might have!'

'My intelligence contacts would know. Don't worry.'

'Are you sure?' Elizabeth looked up.

'You pay me to be sure,' Magnus said with an assured growl, and this time it was Julia who suppressed a smile.

Mabel returned from the hall and clapped her hands together. 'That was Harry Faulkner,' she said. 'Good and bad news. Which would you like first?'

'The bad,' Elizabeth said, at the same moment Julia said, 'The good,' getting a glare from the other woman for her troubles.

'Well, the bad is that we're still snowed in,' she said. 'And the forecast is for more snow tonight. Apparently the snow ploughs are out, but it'll be at least tomorrow before either the roads or the train line are clear. So, you're stuck with us for another night.'

Basil gave a loud bark and a flap of his tail, as though that cheered him up no end.

'And the good?'

Mabel grinned. 'Apparently someone trudged over to the village hall this morning and dug out some dusty tome on local history. It turns out that the village was formed exactly one hundred years ago, in almost exactly the same circumstances. A train—passing through because at that time there wasn't a station here—got delayed by the snow, and the people that got marooned here became the founders of the village.'

'What does that mean for us?' Elizabeth said.

'The village council wants to hold a great party—and since the village was founded right before Christmas, they've decided to double up—and all of you will be the guests of honour.'

'Sounds great,' Julia said.

'Are you insane?' Elizabeth snapped. 'Do you know how it would look for my cred to be spending Christmas in the middle of nowhere? Do you know where I would normally be?'

Julia shook her head, trying to ignore Magnus's grin. 'No. Uh … where?'

'The Ritz! Or the Carlton! Or the Royal Albert Hall! Or … anywhere but Farmersville.'

Julia, maintaining her manners as she had been brought up to, was nevertheless beginning to tire of Elizabeth Trevellian and her neverending petulance.

'You'd better start walking then.'

Elizabeth narrowed her eyes. 'I might.'

'Anyone for more tea?' Mabel asked, holding up the pot with a grin on her face.

~

After breakfast, Julia, Magnus and X helped Mabel to clear the breakfast things away while Elizabeth went back to her room. Joseph reappeared, announced that the wolf enclosure was now safely secured, and then grabbed a leftover piece of toast Mabel had saved for him. Julia excused herself to go back upstairs and take a shower, and was just coming down again when she bumped into Elizabeth, coming out of her room.

'Oh, do be careful. Do you know how much this jacket costs?'

Julia shook her head. 'I don't. But mine was about forty-five pounds from H&M.'

Elizabeth rolled her eyes. 'You know, I used to model for that store? Before my fees got too high for them to afford me.'

'I didn't notice,' Julia said. Then, before she could help herself, she added, 'I thought the models were supposed to smile?'

'What is that supposed to mean?'

Before Julia could reply, Magnus appeared at the end of the hall, head dipped low to avoid hitting the ceiling eaves.

'I've checked the outside, and we're clear,' he said.

'Well, good to see someone's been making themselves useful,' Elizabeth said, giving Julia a withering glare which suggested Julia had unknowingly become a member of staff.

They gathered in the entrance, Basil tugging at his lead, paws raking the front door as Joseph held him back.

'There'll be fresh mince pies waiting when you get back,' Mabel said, then watched from the doorway as Joseph led them all out. A path had been cleared through the snow as far as the front gate, but the road was still buried. A couple of lines of footprints led in either direction, and Joseph followed one, Basil bounding forward, spraying snow everywhere.

'Could you not have cleared this?' Elizabeth snapped at Magnus, as X, hanging back, paused to take a photograph of a pretty robin sitting on a hawthorn branch. The smile on his face dropped when he saw Julia looking, only returning when she gave him a wide grin. X nodded towards Elizabeth, then lifted a finger to his lips.

'You have my apologies,' Magnus was saying. 'I had to chop the wood.'

'Do you know how much these snow boots cost?'

'More than what I am paid?'

'Roughly twice,' Elizabeth said. 'I'd rather not get them dirty.'

'But they are snow boots. They are designed for the dirt.'

Elizabeth groaned. 'Not these. Don't you understand, Magnus? They're not for the snow, are they? They're *fashion.*'

'I am sorry again. I forgot.'

'Don't you know *anything*?'

'I am for security, Mistress. Not for fashion.'

'And it's a good job you're not.'

Julia, walking purposefully at the back, behind X, who kept stopping to take photographs, realised the two of them had slipped back. Further up the road, Basil was setting the pace, With Magnus following behind, Elizabeth stepping in the footprints he made. As X lined up a shot of an icicle hanging from a branch, Julia cleared her throat.

'I know you can talk,' she said.

X gave her a wary look, then a frantic shake of his head. He glanced up the road at Elizabeth's back, then widened his eyes in warning.

'She thinks you can't, doesn't she?'

X smiled and nodded.

'She thinks it's cool that you can't talk, as though that's some kind of gimmick.'

X smiled again, this time nodding frantically.

'You're playing along because she pays well, and it's a career stepping stone.'

X looked surprised. He pouted, then gave a slow nod.

'But really, you're hoping to do something more fulfilling than taking pictures of that self-absorbed airhead, like work for a newspaper, or even a magazine.'

X nodded again.

'Let me guess … BBC?'

X shrugged.

'*The Guardian?*'

Another shrug.

'You were taking pictures of nature, so … *National Geographic?*'

X grinned and gave her a thumbs up.

'Good luck. I hope you can stomach her long enough to build up your portfolio, or whatever it is you photographers do.'

X gave her an okay sign. They walked on a little further, then X paused. He rubbed his chin, then stopped.

'My name is Xavier,' he said in a Spanish accent. 'I'm from Catalonia, in the north of Spain.'

'I've never been, but it looks lovely.'

'Don't tell her,' he said, nodding towards Elizabeth, who was almost out of sight, following Magnus around a corner up ahead. 'She thinks I was born out of a smartphone or something.'

'I think she was born out of a pack of bubblegum.'

Xavier shrugged. 'Don't be too hard on her. She's a product of our times. In many ways, I feel sorry for her.'

'Really?'

'She's lost her grip on reality, that's true. But it's all a charade. She's playing a character, but she's spent so long doing it that she no longer knows what's underneath.'

'That's one way of looking at it. Aren't you playing a character too?'

Xavier smiled. 'Aren't we all?'

Before Julia could reply, a shout came from up ahead. Magnus had stopped and was waving for them to hurry up.

'Duty calls,' Xavier said with a smile. 'Don't forget, I'm a cyborg robot that only communicates via wi-fi.' He tapped the side of his head.

Julia smiled. 'I'll try.'

Everyone had gathered in the pub. Pleased to get away from Elizabeth and her entourage, Julia made a beeline for Kelly and her family, who were drinking hot chocolate at a table by the window. Kelly gave her a warm smile and pulled up a chair for her to sit down.

'Did you survive?' she asked. 'Oh my god, you should see the Grange. It's enormous.'

'Kids couldn't sleep,' Colin said. 'This Lord Andrews guy decided it would be a really good idea to tell some ghost stories in front of the fire. Apparently, some woman threw herself off the roof in the fifteenth century and at night you can sometimes hear her howling. The pipes were so creaky it sounded like she had some friends.'

'It didn't help that he decided to do the whole sheet thing, just for effect,' Kelly said, rolling her eyes.

'The sheet thing?'

'Yeah,' Colin said. 'Crazy old fool waited until we'd all gone to bed, then he puts a bedsheet over his head and runs up and down the halls. Caitlin got up for the toilet and saw him. Mad as a hatter, the old fool. He scared her half to death.'

'I threw an old pot at him,' Caitlin said, lowering her eyes. 'It didn't hit him, but it … broke.'

Kelly patted Caitlin on the shoulder. 'It wasn't your fault, love,' Kelly said. 'He shouldn't have done the sheet thing.'

'Ten grand,' Colin hissed at Julia, so loud even the people on the next table could hear.

Kelly rolled her eyes. 'Still, he took it in good grace, didn't he? Said he enjoyed a good jigsaw puzzle and if he could repair it in time, he'd donate it to the raffle at the Christmas party.'

'The raffle?'

'You'll be staying around for the party, won't you?'

'What party?'

'Christmas Eve.'

'Ah … I don't—'

'You should have seen the size of the beds,' Colin said. 'You could have fitted half a dozen people in them.'

Harry Faulkner appeared from behind the bar, a Christmas hat on his head again, and from the glow to his cheeks clearly already a couple of sherries into the occasion.

'Well, I think everyone's here. Welcome again to Birch Valley. I trust you slept well?' At a few indistinct murmurs, he nodded. 'Good, good. So … ah, the news, because it's not really good or bad, is it? It's just news. And well, it's a little historical. We checked the annals of the village, and it turns out that by some amazing coincidence, this event almost exactly mirrors the events which resulted in the founding of the village one hundred years ago. A delayed train—although a steam train on that occasion—a lot of snow, and exactly twenty stranded people.'

'No wonder the genetics look so good,' Colin muttered.

'So, we've decided we can't let this pass without some ceremony. The village was officially founded on Christmas Eve, 1923, so this year, we've decided to have a huge party. And all of you will be guests of honour.'

Cheers went up in some corners, not quite drowning out the grumbles about getting home from others.

'However, as you've noticed, we're in the middle of a period of quite shocking snowfall, so we're going to need a little help with the preparations.' He gave a nervous grin. 'All hands on deck, and all that.'

'I knew they'd make us earn our keep one way or another,' Colin said.

'Just shush,' Kelly scolded him.

Harry lifted a sheet of paper. 'This is the work roster. You've all been assigned into teams. Of course, if you don't wish to take part, that's fine, but it'll be a couple of days at the very least before rescue services are able to clear the roads, so you might prefer to do something useful.'

A couple of people stuck up their hands. 'I have a doctor's appointment tomorrow!' one woman called. 'I've got tickets for the Cup!' shouted another man.

Harry looked flustered as the complaints bounced against him like flies off a windscreen.

'Okay, look,' he said, 'For those of you who really want to leave, we'll try to mount an expedition to the next village. It will have to be on foot, though, because it'll take some time to clear the snow. Let me consult with the village elders.'

As Harry turned to the bar, leaning into conversation

with Donald the landlord and Stan the station master, Colin chuckled.

'Not decided whose going in the wicker man yet,' he said.

'Oh, stop it,' Kelly said, slapping his arm, although she wore a hint of a smile.

'Dad, what's a wicker man?' Josh asked.

'YouTube it,' Colin said.

'Don't YouTube it!'

'There's no wi-fi,' Josh said.

'Probably just as well,' Kelly said, glancing at Julia.

Feeling rather like a piece of driftwood on a river, with nothing she could do other than go with the flow, Julia listened as Harry talked a while more, then gratefully took a mince pie and a hot chocolate from a tray being carried around. Outside, the sky was a beautiful crystal blue, and despite her initial misgivings, she was warming to the idea of sticking around for a few more days. While it hadn't been her intention when she boarded the train in Brentwell to end up so far outside her comfort zone, it wasn't so bad.

As long as she wasn't in the same team as Elizabeth, things would be fine.

Harry announced that the work activities would begin after lunch, so everyone was free until then to go back to their lodgings or just relax in the pub, getting to know each other. Wanting a bit of fresh air, Julia headed for a door out into a beer garden.

Outside, the sun was warm on her face, the snow so bright she could barely look at it. Tables and chairs were amorphous mounds of white, although a patio had been cleared of snow, and a path down through the garden to a small children's playground, where a group of children now made snowmen or played on swings with lumps of snow occasionally cascading down from the bars overhead.

Lights had been strung around a couple of large potted pine trees on the patio's corners, and along a fence surrounding the garden.

Beyond the pub garden, the village was several meandering lines of quaint houses, snow covered gardens, and even a river still gurgling as it passed under a stone humpback bridge, its banks laden with snow, part of its surface iced over. In the distance, wooded hills rose, hills Julia had only ever seen from the other side, and she realised just how sheltered her world view had always been. So much to see that she had never seen, when, as the crow flew, she was only a few miles from home.

She was still looking at the houses, counting the Christmas trees she could see glowing behind frosty window panes, when she heard familiar voices behind her.

'I know it might sound outlandish, but I will make it worth your while. You do want to save your grandmother's farm, don't you?'

'Look, it's just … I'm not sure about this.'

'It makes perfect sense. We both win. If you're not interested, if money really isn't that important to you, I'll find someone else. I'm not prepared to waste my time while I'm stuck here. I'm losing thousands of subscribers by the day. They need content, and they need content now.'

'I'll think about it.'

'I'll give you until teatime to make your decision.'

'I—'

The door bumped shut. Julia, who had somehow managed to slip behind one of the potted Christmas trees during the conversation, peeked through the branches to see Joseph standing on the other side of the patio, looking confused. Elizabeth had already gone back inside. Joseph stepped down off the patio into the snow, then sat down on the edge, his head in his hands, seemingly oblivious to the cold until a lump of snow dropped off a telephone wire overhead and struck him square on the top of the head. As he yelped and jumped up, swiping the offending lump of snow away, Julia felt a sudden lurch in her chest.

Pack it in. You're thirty-five, not fifteen.

Ignoring the feeling, she shuffled back out of sight, and was relieved when Joseph turned and headed for the door.

She might have avoided an awkward situation altogether, had one of the children on the swings not suddenly shouted, 'Are you playing hide-n-seek? Can we play?'

Joseph turned. He frowned at the children, then looked up at Julia, who was still cowering behind the Christmas tree.

'Oh, hi,' she said, giving him an awkward wave. 'I was just looking at … an … ah … a spiderweb. How … pretty.'

Joseph grinned. 'That's … great.' He looked about to say something else, then shook his head. 'Shall we play?'

'What?'

'Hide-n-seek?'

'Yeah!' shouted a kid from the play area.

Julia smiled, her nervousness melting away. She was desperate to know what Elizabeth and Joseph had been talking about, but it could wait.

'Sure,' she said. 'Why not?'

8

WORK AND PROPHESIES

HIDE-N-SEEK TURNED out to be more fun than Julia had expected, even though until the snow was suitably churned, lines of tracks easily gave them away. Still, after an hour of searching for children hiding behind trees and picnic tables, she was happy to return to the warm confines of the pub, where a lunch of sandwiches and cakes had been laid out.

'So, what did you get?' Kelly asked, as she joined Julia at a window table. 'On the roster, I mean?'

'Oh, I forgot to check. Hang on.'

Harry had pinned the work roster and its allocated groups up on the wall beside the bar. Julia ran a finger down the list of names, looking for her own, disappointed that she wasn't in either the food preparation group, or the costume making group, both of which sounded fun. When she finally found her name and its associated group, her smile dropped.

'Snow clearing,' she said, as she sat back down opposite Kelly.

'Oh, that's too bad,' Kelly said. 'It did look like the

biggest group. Look on the plus side, you'll burn off all this food.'

'What did you get?'

Kelly smiled. 'Child supervision. I suppose it's a mother's natural duty. There's a little playschool in the village which they're opening up this afternoon, so I guess I'll be stuck around watching kids push each other off slides.'

'Hard life.'

'I didn't get a chance to ask you earlier. How was the cottage? I see you were in with that media girl?'

'Elizabeth Trevellian?' Julia rolled her eyes. 'I'm sure I'll get used to her in the end.'

'Is it just that guy and his mother living there?'

'Grandmother.'

'Oh, right. I suppose that's a little more normal, isn't it?'

'What do you mean?'

'Well, living with your mother at his age would mean he's a dependent. But living with his grandmother means he's more likely to be a provider.'

'Is there a label for everything these days?'

Kelly smiled. 'Pretty much. So, what's he like? He's not so hard on the eye, if you know what I mean.'

'What?' Julia felt herself blushing. 'I hadn't … noticed.'

'Yeah, come on. Of course you had. You're practically glowing.'

'I am not!'

'You've been sat down long enough that you can't blame it on a hot flush from the snow. Look, nothing wrong with a bit of a Christmas romance, is there?'

'It's not something I had planned.'

'Just go with the flow. Although I'd get a move on. I think you might have a rival.'

Kelly nodded past Julia's shoulder. Julia glanced around. Joseph was standing at the far end of the bar with Elizabeth beside him. She had one hand on his arm and a desperate look on her face as she said something Julia couldn't hear.

'Don't stare!' Kelly hissed.

Julia turned back, lowering her eyes. 'I wasn't.'

Kelly leaned forwards. 'I'll tell you if anything interesting happens. For what it's worth, he looks like he's trying to get away. Perhaps she wants to buy his soul or something.'

'I doubt that.'

'These social media types don't live in the real world. They care more about getting profile views than they do about mince pies. Isn't that crazy?'

Kelly couldn't help but smile. 'It is a bit.'

'Okay, he's trying to escape, but she's still holding on to his arm. She's actually gripping his jacket ... oh.'

'What?'

'She's angry. She got a bit of snow on her coat. She's looking around for something, maybe a cloth or whatever. Ah, it's that guy with the camera. He's got some kind of spray ... okay, we're safe. Your guy has done a runner, though.'

Julia couldn't help but turn around. Elizabeth was glowering at a slowly closing door, while Xavier stood beside her, dabbing at her coat with a cloth. As Elizabeth turned back, Julia realised she was still staring. Elizabeth met her eyes and scowled just as a grandfather clock in the corner chimed for one o'clock.

'That's our signal,' Kelly said, standing up. 'Work time. What a nightmare, having to watch kids all afternoon.'

Julia glanced at her and smiled. 'Don't strain yourself,' she said, then glanced over her shoulder towards Elizabeth, but the social media starlet had already gone.

~

Clearing snow wasn't so bad. Despite the cold, a bit of exertion kept her warm. And she found that by staying close to Magnus—also on her team—she was able to keep her load relatively light.

Magnus, wearing a Christmas hat, was like an elephant hauling logs. From somewhere he had managed to find a shovel larger than anyone else's, and he cleared snow at the speed of two men with great sweeping movements of his massive arms. And he did it all with a smile on his face, humming along as he worked.

'Have you ever, like, won any prizes?' Julia asked, when she had finally plucked up the courage to start a conversation. 'I mean, for lifting things?'

Magnus smiled. 'World's Strongest Man ... I got to the last heat before the TV stage. I was leading my field, but my shoulder ... I strained a muscle. I don't remember the year. Ninety-seven? And I trialed for the Olympics. Powerlifting. I never quite made it.'

'That's too bad.'

Magnus shrugged, then scooped a massive shovel-load of snow up from the roadside and deposited it into the nearby river, which was doing its best to melt it all away. 'Ah, but I had a good time. You don't need to climb right to the top of the ladder to get the view.'

'No, I suppose not.'

'I have passed the fifty in age,' Magnus said. 'I have travelled to many countries. More than my age's number. I never made the big money or won the big prizes, but I had a good time.'

'And now you work for Elizabeth Trevellian?'

'Yes, on a contract,' Magnus said. 'My agency provides muscle for the famous. I don't know why Ms. Trevellian needs it, to tell the truth. Her critics all live alone, in dark bedrooms. I think she likes the cred. I am a big guy in sunglasses.' He smiled. 'At her request.' He grinned and tapped the glasses, tucked in around his hat. 'I cannot see the road, but if she shows up, I'll have to put them on before she notices.'

'Do you enjoy it?'

Magnus shrugged. 'Working for Ms. Trevellian? It pays the bills. But life on the road means I miss out on life at home.' He stopped shovelling for a moment, leaned on his spade and smiled. 'Two more months until this contract ends, then I'm going home. Back to my dear Sophia.'

'Oh, you're married?'

Magnus smiled. 'Twenty-seven years. Four strong children, all grown and out in the world. I miss them. Very much. My family are dairy farmers, in the northern fjords. But there is no money in the farm these days. Someday soon, though, I will retire, and go back to my farm.'

'You must miss your wife.'

'Oh, yes.' Magnus gave a deep, throaty chuckle. 'But thank the Lord for Facetime.'

Julia couldn't help but smile.

'And how about you, young lady?'

'Me?'

Magnus was still leaning on his spade. 'Yes, you. You like to listen, I noticed yesterday. You know what is said about the listener, don't you?'

Julia shook her head. 'I have no idea.'

Magnus smiled. 'They have the best stories to tell.'

'I don't have any stories.'

'Oh, you do. You came here on the journey. What was your journey?'

'I was going home for Christmas, that's all. My parents live in Olive Hill, the next stop on the line.'

'And you're travelling alone?'

'Yes, look, why do people keep asking me that?'

'I mean no offence. It's Christmas. No one wants to be alone at Christmas.'

'I'm sorry. It's just a bit of a sensitive subject.'

Magnus smiled again. 'You can call me Uncle Magnus, then tell me all about it.'

Julia shrugged. 'There's not a lot to tell. I've been living in Brentwell since I graduated from Exeter University. I work in an office. Company insurance. I type numbers into a screen. It's easy work.'

'What do you like best about this work?'

Julia shrugged. 'The office has a free coffee machine.'

'No secret lover at the job?'

'No!' Julia hacked at a pile of snow with her spade. 'I went on a date with someone once, but that was about five years ago. I'm kind of in the middle now. All the other guys are either married middle-managers or kids hitting the clubs.'

'You feel set adrift, like on a raft upon the river?'

'Not exactly. I had a boyfriend.'

'Oh. Wedding bells?'

'He's in prison.'

'Why?'

Julia sighed. 'He stole my car and sold it. Then I found out later he'd stolen a lot of other cars, and sold them too.'

'And this fool could find no honest work?'

'It seems not.'

'There is only the wheel,' Magnus said. 'And we all must push the wheel up the hill. Sometimes the wheel is heavy. But we must push. If we let go of the wheel, the wheel will roll down the hill.'

Julia nodded. 'That's right,' she said. 'I think.'

'And what do you think about beyond this Christmas?'

'I haven't really thought about it. I'll go back to Brentwell, start back at work in January, and take it from there.'

'Typing the numbers?'

'That's right.'

'You must visit my farm. My Sofia, she will take care of you.'

'Ah, thanks. I'll think about it.'

Magnus dug his spade into a pile of snow and seemingly lifted the entire mound into the air. Julia stared as he unloaded it into the river.

'Thinking does not push the wheel,' Magnus said. 'Nor does it move the snow.'

At the very least, Julia felt like she had earned her dinner by the time Harry Faulkner came bustling past a couple of hours later to announce that work was over for the day. Julia, exhausted, but having enjoyed herself more than she might have expected, trailed the rest of her group back to the pub, where, in Harry's words, 'Good job drinks and snacks' had been set out on a wide trestle table. Julia grabbed a warm mince pie and poured herself a cup of hot chocolate, wincing at the hint of something alcoholic hiding inside, then sat down on a corner table with a view outside.

It was just after four o'clock, and the sun had already dropped behind the hills to the west. Her team had spent the afternoon clearing the main road through the village, shovelling the snow into piles which had later turned into snowmen or mini slopes for kids with sledges. Another team had been responsible for stringing fairy lights through the bushes and shrubs of front gardens, and now they all began to blink on, turning Birch Valley into a glittering Christmas village.

There were worse places to spend Christmas, she figured, as she spotted Kelly and Colin across the street, putting the finishing touches to a snowman while Josh and Caitlin pushed stones into its chest and added sticks for arms.

'Your time will come, dear,' came an old woman's voice from behind her, and Julia let out a gasp of fright. Edwina O'Fara, in full mystic gear with a beaded headscarf and necklace made of pearls and feathers leaned over the table. 'But not without trial, I fear.'

'Edwina, leave her alone,' Reginald said, trying to pull his wife away.

'The bells of a church will leave your heart in a lurch, but if you bide your time, what you want … you will find.'

'Edwina, come on, let's get some mince pies before they run out.'

Edwina ignored him. She leaned over where Julia was cowering, and put an arm on Julia's shoulder. 'Heed my words, dear. The cards are never wrong.'

'Uh … sure.'

Reginald succeeded in pulling his wife away, leading her back to the food table, where, from the relieved grin on his face, it seemed there were enough mince pies left.

Julia looked down at her hands, surprised to see they were trembling. What had the old crone been on about? Not without trial? The bells of a church?

Birch Valley had a little church up the street, its spire just visible above the nearest houses. Suddenly feeling an urge to be alone, Julia got up and headed outside, zipping up her coat and pulling the hood up over her head. She pulled on her gloves and stuffed her hands into her pockets anyway, the air chilling quickly now the sun was gone.

Stars were blinking on, the moon visible above the nearest hills as Julia wandered up through the village. Most of the roads had been cleared, the sun having melted off the dusting left behind, so she found herself walking on tarmac for the first time since she had boarded the train yesterday afternoon. It felt a little strange, lifting her mood a little, but when she came to a junction where a sign pointing left said *Olive Hill 6 Miles*, a wall of snow blocked her way in that direction, piled three feet deep, and although she was able to clamber over the top of it, the continuing road was knee-deep in slowly thickening, icing snow. A hundred paces or so past the junction a tree had come down, so she reluctantly gave up any chance of escape.

Instead, she headed on up the cleared road through the village, cheering up a little when a group of kids briefly engaged her in a snowball fight, then shortly after when she heard the sound of bad Christmas karaoke through an open living room window. By the time she reached the church, she was skipping a little, and not just because of the cold.

Lights shone through the windows. Edwina O'Fara's words reverberated in her ears. Perhaps it would be best to stay outside, but something was compelling her to go in, to see if there was any truth to the old mystic's words.

Grey stone walls rose in front of her. All around, angled grave stones poked up out of the snow. The path had been trodden down, but fresh footprints were visible leading up to the porch. Light shone under the heavy wooden door.

Julia paused inside the porch, leaning against the door. Voices clearly came from inside, but she couldn't make out words. Turning the large metal door handle, she eased the door open wide enough to slip through.

At first, she found herself smiling. The church had been decorated for Christmas, and looked positively delightful, with lights, wreaths and tinsel hung from the walls. A large, ornate Christmas tree stood in the centre at the back, with another near the front by the pulpit. Gentle classical Christmas music played quietly from hiding speakers, and Julia found herself inside before she knew it. While she would never consider herself religious, there was definitely a hint of Christmas magic in the air inside the church. As she stood by the Christmas tree at the back, examining ornate, hand carved wooden decorations of stars and bells, movement caught her eye. She looked up as a vicar appeared out of a side door, pursued by a woman in jarring white.

'Look, we just can't squeeze it in,' he said. 'There's too much other stuff going on. You'll have to wait until after Christmas.'

'You don't understand,' the woman said. Julia stared, recognising Elizabeth Trevellian's voice. 'It has to be done before Christmas. Did you not hear how much I'm willing to donate? See that bucket over there? Do you like having a leaking roof?'

'I can't just accommodate a wedding at four days' notice.'

'Five. I told you, the twenty-fourth.'

The vicar, a man in his sixties with a shiny bald head but eyebrows so bushy it looked like they had collected his hair as it fell, flapped his hands.

'It's the evening of the nineteenth, it'll be the twentieth in a few hours. That makes it more or less four days.'

'You're just being pedantic.' Elizabeth followed the vicar to the pulpit and stood at the bottom while he went up and flicked over a few pages of a large bible.

'Don't you think it's a little inappropriate to plan a wedding on the morning of the village's hundred-year anniversary?'

Elizabeth shook her head. 'It'll be the showpiece of the whole event. The anniversary celebration can double as a wedding reception. I want the whole village invited. That's the point.'

The vicar turned to her. 'I thought the whole point was to be joined in holy matrimony with a man you love?'

Elizabeth rolled her eyes. 'This isn't the nineteen fifties.'

The vicar descended from the pulpit and took off across the church, Elizabeth trailing behind. 'I'm not prepared to officiate over a sham wedding,' he said, wandering back and forth, seemingly just trying to get away from the woman quite literally walking in his shadow. 'This isn't Las Vegas.'

'From the cracks in the walls and the water dripping through the roof, I'd say it won't be anywhere soon,' Elizabeth said. 'That's why you need to officiate my wedding. Can you really afford to turn down the donation that I'm offering?'

The vicar stopped walking. He put his hands on a pillar and rested his head against the cold stone. 'No,' he said. 'I can't.'

'So, it's agreed then. We'll hold the wedding ceremony on the morning of the twenty-fourth, Christmas Eve, followed by the village's celebration which will double as my wedding reception. It shouldn't be a problem to have them change the itinerary a little to accommodate my needs.'

The vicar sighed. He lifted his head, looking past a smugly grinning Elizabeth towards the front rows of pews. For the first time Julia realised there was another person sitting there, in the front row, quietly watching proceedings.

'A marriage involves two people,' the vicar said, giving Elizabeth a sharp glare. 'What do you think, sir? Do you want to marry this woman you just met in a little over four days' time?'

The figure shifted, and Julia's breath caught as the man lifted his head, tilting it just enough for her to recognise him.

'Yes,' croaked Joseph, then lowered his head again in apparent resignation, while Julia, having heard enough, made a hasty retreat, slipping back out of the church and into the night, where the first flakes of a fresh snow had just begun to fall.

GHOSTS AND KARAOKE

'Hi, Mum.'

'Oh, hi, love. How are you coping?'

Julia stared at the wall of her bedroom. 'I'm surviving. I kind of wish I was at home, though. It's not the same here, really.'

'You sound so down, love. Cheer up, it's nearly Christmas. The girls haven't trashed your room yet, although they were having a pillow fight in there earlier.'

Julia winced. 'I suppose it could be worse.'

'Don't worry, we'll see you soon. Enjoy your little adventure while you can, though. You might make some new friends.'

'Yeah, maybe.'

'You might even meet someone special. After that last one you deserve a little luck.'

'I doubt it, Mum.'

'You never know.'

Julia shook her head. 'Really, it's not going to happen.'

'You should be more positive about things.'

Julia thought about the conversation she had overheard in the church. 'I'm trying,' she said.

'Julia!' came Mabel's voice up the stairs. 'Are you coming, dear?'

'Mum, I've got to go,' Julia said. 'See you soon, I hope.'

'Bye, love. Love you. Take care.'

'And you, Mum.'

Julia hung up, then set the phone down beside her bed. Mabel called her again, and Julia briefly wondered if she should make up some kind of excuse to miss dinner. A dodgy mince pie, maybe? Perhaps the flu? Or maybe leprosy? Anything to avoid Elizabeth's smug face. However, after an afternoon of digging snow and an evening of aimless walking through cold, snowy streets, she was starving, and while her resolve might want one thing, her stomach shouted louder.

'Coming,' she called.

Downstairs, the seating arrangement of previous mealtimes had been rearranged. Magnus still sat at one end, but Joseph now sat at the other end, with Elizabeth uncomfortably close on his left. Julia was next to Magnus with Mabel across from her, with Xavier sitting between Julia and Joseph.

Mabel had cooked a mouthwatering roast beef, complete with piles of vegetables and trimmings. Open bottles of wine stood tantalisingly close. Julia sat on her hands to stop herself from grabbing and swigging directly from the nearest bottle.

As soon as Mabel had finished dishing out the food, Elizabeth stood up. She tapped a wine glass with a spoon, a jarring sound around a table that was already silent. Only Basil reacted, lifting his head from his basket and letting out a low moan.

'I'd like to make an announcement,' Elizabeth said,

although from complete lack of reaction around the table, Julia was certain she was the only one who didn't already know. 'After a whirlwind romance, Jason and myself have decided to get married.'

'Joseph,' Joseph said, briefly looking up, before lowering his head again.

'There's no need to worry about trivial matters,' Elizabeth snapped. 'What's important is our love.' She reached down in an attempt to pat him on the shoulder, but he had leaned over to pass a piece of beef to Basil, and instead she just made an awkward pumping motion in midair. Mabel sighed and looked away. Xavier took a picture. Magnus glanced at Julia and offered a smile of solidarity.

'Congratulations,' Julia muttered.

'I'd like to propose a toast,' Elizabeth said, lifting a glass of water. 'To myself and … ah … Joseph.'

Everyone except Xavier—who was holding his camera—lifted their glasses. Julia muttered something even she couldn't hear and then swigged down half her glass of wine. It actually made her feel better. Magnus, perhaps noticing her discomfort, reached over and topped it up.

'Yes,' Elizabeth was saying, still standing up. 'I know you're probably all wondering how we could find love so quickly in such a little village in the middle of nowhere, but I guess that's just what snow and a little Christmas magic can do for you.' She fiddled nervously with a loose strand of hair, then frowned at Xavier, whom Julia realised was filming. 'Would you like me to do that again?'

Xavier shook his head, then mouthed something.

'Yes, natural is good,' Elizabeth said. Then, shaking her head, she cleared her throat and continued, 'And what a joining of worlds indeed. A simple farmer with one of the world's most famous online faces. A no one with … a someone. Proof right here on my channel that love can overcome all adversity. And I want all of you to be there for my special moment, which will of course be streamed live.'

'Any chance you could sit down, dear, and eat your lettuce before it goes warm,' Mabel said.

Elizabeth rolled her eyes. 'We'll cut that bit … so, on December 24th, the event of the year. One that will usurp even Christmas itself. The marriage of … Elizabeth Trevellian.'

She continued to hold the pose for a few seconds until Xavier lifted a hand and made an OK sign. Elizabeth let out a sigh, nodded, and sat down. Ignoring Joseph completely, she stuffed a leaf of lettuce into her mouth, then stood up again.

'Thank you for the meal, Grandmother,' she said to Mabel. 'Oh, that sounded so strange! I must go and exfoliate. X, I'll need you to film it. If we still can't get any connection for the live stream, we'll prerecord to release it later.'

She left without another word, heading out of the kitchen. Xavier checked that she had gone before stuffing a large slice of beef into his mouth.

'Don't worry,' Mabel said, as Xavier gave her a regretful smile and then stood up. 'I'll heat it up again later.'

Almost as soon as the door to the hall had closed behind him, Joseph stood up. Not making eye contact with anyone, he muttered, 'I need to go and feed the wolves,' and hurried out.

A couple of moments of silence passed, during which Julia tried to concentrate on her food. The beef was perfect. The potatoes exquisite. The broccoli was firm to the bite, lightly salted—

A chuckle from the end of the table made her look up. Magnus, a huge slice of beef speared on his fork, was trying to contain himself.

'I think the snow fall too heavy on people's heads,' he said. 'All sense has been squeezed out.'

Mabel speared a carrot and popped it into her mouth. 'I don't know what to say,' she said. 'He dropped it on me this afternoon. I wasn't aware that he'd even spoken to the lass up until that point.' She sighed. 'I wasn't convinced the girl was even human. I'm even less sure now.'

'I hear from the man in the pub that tonight is karaoke,' Magnus said. 'Who will join me in a song?'

'Karaoke?' Julia said, still trying to get over the news of Joseph's forthcoming wedding.

'You take the mic, and you rock the mic,' Magnus said. 'Do you enjoy to sing the song in the shower? It's just the same.'

Julia smiled. 'I think I get the idea.'

Mabel stood up. 'Let's go,' she said.

After they had finished eating and cleared up, they headed out. Having seen no further sign of Elizabeth, Xavier, or Joseph, they left them behind. It had begun to snow again, however, so Magnus lifted Mabel and perched her on his shoulders as he trudged through the snow like a marching robot, leaving Julia struggling to keep up. The main road into the village had been cleared during the day, however, so the fresh snow made a welcome and delightful crunch under their boots. Up ahead, the village greeted them with strings of fairy lights strung across the streets, and as they turned a corner to find the pub in front of them, the muffled sound of music came from inside. Magnus set

Mabel down, and they went together, Mabel opening the door to reveal a party in progress. Locals and maroonees alike twirled and danced in the middle of the bar. Two laughing women held a limbo pole up for people carrying sloshing drinks to shimmy under.

'It is like being on the holiday,' Magnus said, glancing at Julia. 'I will order the drinks. Bartender!'

'Hey, you!' Kelly said, pushing her way through the crowd. 'Glad you could make it. Colin, dear of him, offered to do the child watch for the evening. You just missed a round of peach schnapps. It's like Tenerife all over again.'

'I'm ready for the next round,' Julia said.

'Been that kind of day, has it?'

Julia gave a grim nod. 'Something like that.'

The party, however, did its best to lift her mood, especially when the karaoke began. An old grey-haired man in a tweed jacket and wearing a monocle got up and did a rather stuffy version of White Christmas, to which the locals all politely clapped. The visitors just shared perplexed looks among each other.

'That's him,' Kelly hissed, as the old man handed the microphone back to Don behind the bar. 'Lord Andrews. They all have to be nice to him because he owns most of the land round here. Seems like a jovial fellow though. It wouldn't surprise me if he does the sheet thing again when he gets home. The kids are wised up to it now, though.'

After a group of locals did a rather ironic version of *I've Got a Brand New Combine Harvester*, Magnus got up and pulled off a pretty good rendition of Arnie and the Terminators' classic *I'll be Back*. With his sunglasses and leather jacket, he looked straight off the film set. Julia was still laughing when Kelly pulled on her arm.

'Come on. I don't get out much, and I'm not drunk enough to do this on my own.'

'What?'

Julia found herself dragged to the front of the bar where a small stage had been erected. A microphone was pushed into her hand and she stared at a TV monitor on the floor as the titles for *You're the One That I Want* from Grease appeared on the screen.

'You want John or Olivia?' Kelly asked.

'Ah….'

'Okay, I'll be John.'

Kelly was like a dog let off a leash, twisting and jiving as the song came on. Julia, feeling a little overawed, did her best to hang in there, slowly growing in enthusiasm as the song progressed. As Kelly belted out her half of the vocals, Julia found herself growing in confidence. It wasn't like she didn't know the song; she had to have seen the film a hundred times. And when she looked out at the crowd and realised the smiles and cheers were encouraging her rather than waiting for her to fail, she felt a surge of confidence.

As the song ended and the crowd cheered, she held her microphone aloft, holding the pose. Beside her, Kelly howled with excitement. They gave each other a high five, then climbed down from the stage.

'So,' Julia said, breathless. 'What song are we going to do next?'

They had to wait a while before they got another chance. Evidently Birch Valley wasn't usually the party capital of Devon, but with a sudden influx of new blood, it was taking on the mantle, and the locals didn't want to be left out. A procession of Christmas songs, fifties classics, and a few dodgy eighties hits followed, before Kelly hauled

Julia up for a duet version of *We Are the Champions*. By now, a lot of people had tired and gone home, but there was time for one more drink before Magnus took the stage first for a duet with Mabel of *I've Got You, Babe,* then a blistering solo version of an Iron Maiden song, which left the few remaining patrons wide-eyed with both awe and terror.

'I think that we will not need to worry about being jumped on our way back,' he said with a grin as he sat back down.

Even so, he insisted on first taking Mabel home, then returning alone to escort Kelly and Julia.

'Colin's going to kill me,' Kelly slurred as they walked up a long, winding driveway towards the Grange. Julia was yet to see the local manor house, but was too tired to get excited as lights gradually appeared through the trees. 'I promised I'd be back by ten.'

'It's only eleven thirty,' Julia said, then giggled as her own words came out in a slurred rush.

'One forty-five,' Magnus corrected. 'These farm people drink like the fish. In fact, they drink like the whale.'

'Oh gosh, that late?'

Magnus chuckled. 'It's nearly the Christmas,' he said. 'Do not worry.'

They came around the last bend in the driveway, Magnus supporting Kelly on one side and Julia on the other, while still managing to keep a torch directed at the road in front. The manor house rose ahead of them as the driveway arched around in front, circling around a circular stone fountain with a rearing horse in the middle and a lump of ice on its head where the water would usually spout from. The house, three floors of Edwardian elegance, had a wide stone staircase leading up to its front doors. Julia felt a pang of jealousy as she looked up at several illuminated windows on the top floor.

'The Christmas tree in the hall is a marvel,' Kelly said. 'Do you think Lord Andrews would mind if I took you in for a quick look?'

'You may have the opportunity to ask,' Magnus said, pointing at a white shape detaching itself from the shadows beside the stairs. 'And I think to please him, it might be good to act afraid.'

'Oooooh!' came a howl, followed by a cackle of drunken laughter, as the bedsheet ghost came tearing towards them.

'How long do you think he's been waiting for us?' Kelly said.

'He has the snow on the top of the head,' Magnus said. 'I think the man is out of his mind.'

'Just play along,' Kelly said. Then, as the running figure approached, she let out a yelp of fright and ran off, almost losing her footing as she turned, before managing to right herself. Julia watched her for a moment, then turned and followed, with Magnus close behind.

'Help!' Kelly cried, not loud enough to wake anyone inside the house. 'Help us, someone.'

'There is the ghost on my tail!' Magnus shouted. 'I do not like the ghost!'

'Help,' Julia called, joining in, as she followed Kelly in a circuit of the stone fountain. They did one more loop with Lord Andrews in pursuit, before the ghost-obsessed peer came to a gasping stop. He pulled off the bedsheet in one sudden moment, leaving it on the fountain's stone ledge, then looked up at them, a wide smile on his face as he gasped for breath.

'Goodness me,' he said. 'It's like being a child again. You didn't know it was me, did you? You really thought this place was haunted.'

Julia, Kelly and Magnus all nodded, muttering affirmatives.

Lord Andrews tapped the side of his nose. 'Let's keep my little secret, shall we? Who doesn't like a bit of a local legend, right? Now, who's up for a quick apéritif? I have some delightful brandies down in the cellar. Although, rumour has it that the cellar might be haunted....'

They were unable to resist an offer made by a lord, and it was a good hour later when Magnus and Julia finally left, heading back down the long driveway and then through the village to finally reach Chapel Cottage. Julia felt weary beyond words, but as they reached the house, she faintly heard Joseph's voice coming from around the side of the house. Magnus excused himself and went inside, leaving Julia standing outside the front porch, straining her ears to hear.

'That's it. Just a little more. Good girl. Good ... girl!'

Her brain couldn't compute what she was hearing, so she just gave a tired shake of her head. Then, with the alcohol still maintaining a tenuous hold on her senses, she shouted out, 'Have a happy wedding!', just a little more angrily than she had intended.

Joseph's voice had gone quiet. Julia suddenly realising what she had said, clapped a hand over her mouth, but it was too late. Aware that anything she did from now on would only make matters worse, she hurried into the house, hoping that when she woke up in the morning, the snow would have melted, and she could go home.

10

HONOURS AND SPIES

SHE WOKE UP LATE. Less hungover than she might have thought, she was nevertheless in desperate need of some coffee. Pulling back the curtains, she found herself presented with a fresh snowstorm, the world outside a swirling mass of white. With a sigh she headed downstairs.

Mabel was in the kitchen, whistling to herself as she washed up the breakfast things.

'I'm sorry about yesterday,' Julia mumbled, sidling up to Mabel like a naughty schoolgirl. 'Things got a little out of hand.'

Mabel turned, a wide grin on her face. 'Oh, my dear, that's the best night out I've had in thirty years. I haven't done a tequila slammer since my nephew's wedding. I can still taste the lemon. It couldn't have gone better unless I'd scored, but there's not much chance of that round here, even though I got my hopes up for a while there with all the fresh faces.'

Julia momentarily wondered if she was still in bed and this was all part of a surreal dream, then she smelled the coffee in the pot and realised that no, Mabel had in fact just said what Julia thought she had. Perhaps it might be good to get an early night tonight.

'Sit down, dear, and I'll get you some breakfast. The others all went out early this morning. Up to the church, I think. All of them except Joseph, who's up with the wolves. You know we had pups last night?'

Julia blinked. 'Puppies?'

'Wolf offspring are just pups. Bella gave birth last night.'

'Bella?'

'That's our female. Joseph sat out there with her all night, bless him. He was worried about the snow closing in again, but everything went fine. We have nine little wolf pups to name.'

'*Nine?*'

'They're adorable. Well, they currently resemble sausages with legs, but it won't be long before they're scampering about the place.'

'Wow. Ah … congratulations. Where's Joseph now?'

'He's still out there. He camped out in the shed last night.' Mabel sighed. 'I did feel a little guilty that instead of helping I went out on the lash, so to speak, but he's still young whereas I'll probably die soon.'

'Ah, right.'

'Cornflakes or muesli? Or both?'

'Ah—'

'Or a fry up? Or both?'

'I—'

'I'll tell you what. You just sit there and keep me company for a while, and I'll organise you a breakfast special.'

'You really don't need to go to so much trouble.'

Mabel wouldn't be dissuaded, however, so Julia had to content herself with a couple of strong cups of coffee while Mabel filled the table around her with far more food than she needed. As soon as she started to eat, however, she found she was starving. Perhaps that was what came from being chased by a lord in a bedsheet in the middle of the night.

'So,' Julia said, as she swallowed a piece of bacon. 'Where are the others?'

'Oh, you mean her ladyship?' Mabel's smile dropped. 'She's taken her long-suffering entourage up to the church to plan *her* wedding.'

Perhaps Julia was still a little drunk from the night before, but she found herself being uncharacteristically forward as she said, 'Aren't you pleased for him?'

'Pleased? Are you out of your mind? He's only known the girl for forty-eight hours. And what a hideous choice. I'd rather he married Bella than that fiend.'

'Bella … the wolf?'

'Although I'm sure Barry would be a little jealous.'

'Right … but she's so pretty.'

Mabel leaned forward, eyes narrowing over her spectacles. 'She's pretty on the outside,' she said. 'But she's so vacuous you could pop her like a balloon.'

Julia tended to agree, but felt it necessary to play devil's advocate. 'But how can you tell after just a couple of days? Perhaps there's more to her than you realise.'

'Do you really think so?'

'Well, no….'

'Exactly. I have porcelain dolls in the living room with more personality, and less likelihood of showing up in a horror movie.'

Again, Julia began to wonder if she was actually still dreaming, so she speared a lump of sausage, dipped it in some brown sauce and stuffed it into her mouth.

Nope, she was definitely awake.

'But Joseph is a nice person,' she said a little awkwardly as she chewed the sausage. 'He must have seen something we haven't.'

Outside, the snow had stopped. A little robin landed on a bird feeder hanging outside the kitchen window, pulled a piece of nut free and then flew away again. A clock in the hallway chimed ten o'clock.

'He's a good man is my grandson,' Mabel said. 'I know exactly what he's doing. And it has nothing to do with love.'

Julia wasn't sure what else she could say, so she quietly finished as much of the food as she could—too much, if she were honest about it, but it was Christmas, and she couldn't resist a cheeky mince pie from a bowl in the table's centre after finishing her fry up—then excused herself to go and get dressed. A few minutes later she came back downstairs and volunteered for whatever housework Mabel needed doing. She wanted to ask more about Joseph, but at that moment the door opened and Elizabeth came marching in. With her coat flecked with snow and an angry scowl on her face, she only needed a sceptre made of ice to be a thoroughly convincing snow queen of legend.

'That troublesome little man,' she said, as Xavier, following in behind, squatted low to take a picture of Elizabeth framed against the kitchen backdrop. Magnus came in last, carrying a cloth which he used to wipe snowy footprints off the flagstone floor, before giving Mabel an apologetic look.

'What happened, dear?' Mabel said.

'I simply wished for some cameras and a lighting system to be installed in the church,' Elizabeth said, sniffing as though she might cry, before leaning over and hissing to Xavier, 'How did that look?'

'That's a shame, dear.'

'It would be quite alright for you to call me daughter,' Elizabeth said, abruptly switching personalities to something so closely resembling human that Julia was quite stunned. 'After all, we will soon be family, won't we?'

'But Joseph isn't my son,' Mabel said.

'Stop being so trivial. Ah, you're awake. Good.'

Julia, used to being ignored, was surprised to find that Elizabeth was now staring at her. 'Um, yes?'

'We need to talk about your dress.'

'My … dress?'

'You're the Maid of Honour.'

'The—'

'Do you really need to repeat everything I say?'

Julia glanced at Mabel, who, rather than irate as Julia might have expected, looked rather amused. Perhaps she thought she was still asleep too.

'The maid of … honour?'

'Yes, and I'm sure it truly is an honour for you. Obviously, I would prefer to have asked one of my online friends or perhaps run a competition to decide the lucky person, but time is short and there aren't a lot of options around here. Therefore, you'll have to do. I will of course make it worth your while with a week's holiday, fully paid for. Where would you like to go? France? Spain? Italy?

'Home,' muttered Julia.

'Well, you're not the only one, but let's not be selfish, shall we?' Elizabeth turned her crosshairs back to Mabel. 'And I'll need to borrow the wolf. The female one.'

'Whatever for?'

'I need a ring bearer. And it's been proven time and again that having some kind of animal perform the deed gets you ten to fifteen percent more likes and five percent more shares.'

'Can't you use Basil? Although there's a possibility he might eat it.'

'The beast must be female. It's symbolic.'

'You can't use Bella. She's only just given birth. The pups are nursing.'

Elizabeth gave a tired huff. 'Can't you put them in an incubator or something? It'll only be for a couple of hours. She won't need to appear at the reception. Oh, did I mention that Lord Andrews has allowed us to use the Grange? I've invited everyone from the village.'

'Is that right?'

'What a great centerpiece for the anniversary celebration,' Elizabeth said. 'You're all so lucky. And while I wouldn't quite consider myself the same, it's a sign of one's versatility to be able to adapt to the needs of each new situation.'

Without waiting for an answer, she hurried off down the hall to her room, Xavier trailing in her wake. Magnus gave the two ladies a shrug and an apologetic smile, then announced he would go out and clear the fresh snow from the path.

Julia helped Mabel finish clearing up the kitchen, then offered to go and help Magnus. Once outside, however, she found the path and the road outside already cleared, and no sign of the giant Norwegian. Instead, Julia headed around the side of the house and followed a line of tracks down a path that led through a gap in the hedge. A small shed-like building stood beyond, with a fence stretching away on the other side. Barry was running back and forth along the inside of the fence, pursued by Basil, whose fur had collected enough of the snow that from a distance he resembled a baby polar bear.

The shed door was shut. As Julia approached, the muffled sound of two male voices were just about audible.

'They will grow up big and strong like their mother.' Magnus's voice.

'I hope so. It's a shame we'll have to sell most of them, but wolf-husky mixes are greatly sought after. The money will help.' So, that was where Joseph had been all morning.

'She does not pay you enough for the gift of your soul?' Magnus chuckled. 'Maybe if you offer to cut out your heart for her to eat?'

'It might hurt the business even more,' Joseph said. 'My grandmother has a fine reputation, and by marrying Elizabeth, I could be ruining it. People aren't stupid. They know it's fake.'

'She commands power over many stupid people, 'Magnus said. 'You need to fake your love.'

'I'm trying, but I just can't get my head around it.'

'Look at the wolf. She has the love for the babies. Look at her eyes. You look at her like that, maybe you feel the love.'

'I'll try. How long for, though? A week, a month? A year?'

'Until she finds her next soul to steal,' Magnus said with a chuckle.

Julia tried to take a step back, but caught her foot on a rock hidden under the snow. She slipped, nudging a tree, which in turn showered her with snow, then raked its bouncing branches against the shed roof.

'A spy,' came Magnus's voice.

Julia turned and ran. She heard the shed door opening, but didn't look back. She ran back to the house, then out along the path on to the road, turning left and running until she reached as far as the snow had been cleared.

She was sick of this place, and its weirdness. All she wanted to do was go home.

Nearby was a sign at the end of a buried junction,

indicating Birch Valley back the way she had come, and Olive Hill straight ahead. The snow had piled up here, a small mountain across the road, but as Julia climbed up and over the top, she found it wasn't nearly as deep on the other side. A car wouldn't be able to make it, and even a tractor might struggle, but a human, with a bit of willpower, could manage.

Ahead of her, the road wound down into a valley, then rose again, disappearing into a stand of woodland. The snow came up to her knees, but it wasn't like she could get lost. All she had to do was follow the road, and in a couple of hours she would be home.

She had swapped numbers with Kelly so that they could keep in touch, and perhaps after the snow was gone, she might stop in to thank Mabel for her hospitality. She had left her suitcase behind with most of her things inside, but she put it out of her mind. The snow would be gone in a couple of days. She could pick it up after Christmas perhaps. There was nothing she couldn't live without.

Her decision made, she clenched her fists, realising for the first time that she had forgotten her gloves. It didn't matter; she had pockets. And she wasn't going to let any trivial matter stop her.

Glaring at the road ahead as though it were a personal enemy, she set out, trudging through the snow, determined to make it home.

It was a good job she had eaten a big breakfast, but with a bit of luck she would be there in time for lunch.

11

SECOND THOUGHTS

THE SUN overhead was almost warm, and it was doing its best to turn the fallen snow into a type of glue Julia had never experienced. Having neglected to bring either her watch or her phone—not to mention her purse—she had no idea of the time, nor how far she had gone, but she was exhausted before she had even reached the bottom of the neighbouring valley. As she gathered her strength for the climb up the hill, she reflected on how different the countryside became when you were facing adversity. On a fine day she would no doubt have passed houses and farm lanes, perhaps even a few dog walkers or even horse riders. Now she felt like all human existence had been erased from the world, except for the roads and the hedgerows hemming her in. Through field gateways she glimpsed distant farms and even a small town, but nothing ever seemed to get any closer. Where were all the quaint cottages that always seemed to line the roads, the lanes leading down to secluded farms? There was just the road, and the hedgerows, and the snow.

She began to give serious consideration to the idea of

turning back. After all, her own tracks were the only ones in the snow behind her, and all she had to do was follow them. She had probably only gone a mile, although the sweat down her back and the ache in her thighs made it feel like it was about twenty-five.

For a long time in her life, Julia had felt like a bland, modern version of Huckleberry Finn, one floating downriver with no way of returning, albeit without a friend, a pole, an aim, nor much in the way of any adventure. A couple of failed relationships. A half-decent holiday to Corsica with a couple of friends where she'd briefly snogged a local. A promotion to group leader only for an internal company reshuffle to remove her title even if her pay grade remained. A cat. A car she had liked before it had been stolen and trashed in the process.

Her little stopover in Birch Valley hadn't been supposed to happen. She should be standing in her mother's kitchen right now, moaning to her sister over a glass of wine about how Cassandra and Ebony had cut their toenails and not cleaned it up, or how Cousin Albert's hippy music kept her awake at night. She should have been stuck in a trivial variation of last year's Christmas—and the year before, and the year before that, going back as long as she could remember.

Then, out of nowhere, she had been gifted something unique. A late train, random new friends, sharing a house with a crazy internet influencer. Wolves. A guy with a weird name. A Norwegian strongman and a crazy lord who chased people with a bedsheet over his head.

And a young, rather confused man whom she found herself thinking about rather more often than she would like.

And she was running away?

She stopped dead in the snow.

'What on earth am I doing?' she said aloud. 'I should be loving every minute of this.'

She had just crested a rise, and there, in the distance, she recognised the tower of Olive Hill's little church. Her parents' house was tucked in behind it, just out of sight, but in an hour, perhaps two, she could be standing outside.

With a smile, she turned away, shaking her head.

A couple more days and she would be home anyway, but let her mother and sister deal with Cousin Albert and his clan for now.

'I'm having an adventure,' she said.

It wasn't much easier going back the way she had come, because the wells in the snow that her boots had made had crusted up in the sun around the edges while turning to sludge on the inside, so after a while she stopped retracing her steps and simply created a new, fresh line parallel to the one she had already made.

Now, though, as she headed back, she felt a slowly rising panic. She seemed to have gone much further than she had thought. The sun was dipping towards the distant hills, and her stomach was growling with hunger. She was long past lunchtime, and it was literally the shortest day of the year, dark around four o'clock. She had no source of light, and clouds were moving in from the east, threatening yet more snow.

'I could die out here,' she muttered, then louder: 'I could *die* out here.'

She tried to run, but after nearly falling on her face realised it was literally impossible. She had tears in her eyes, but it was starting to get cold, her breath puffing out in front of her. The resolve she had felt when she turned back had melted away, and she started to doubt herself all over again. She stopped, turning back, wondering if there was still time to make it to Olive Hill, but she had made her choice. If her fate was a cold, lonely death in the snow, then so be it.

She looked up … and saw three figures coming around the corner in the distance, two humans and one rather large dog. One human towered over the other, and as they spotted her they lifted their hands above their heads and began to wave.

'Julia! Julia!'

'I'm here!' she shouted, jumping up and down. 'I'm right here! And I'm coming back!'

Both Magnus and Joseph looked flustered as they reached her a few minutes later. Joseph reached her first, pulling her into an awkward hug before stepping back and giving her a bashful smile.

'We were worried,' he said. 'You've been gone for hours.'

Julia wiped tears out of her eyes. 'I just … went for a walk. I wanted to see if I could get home, but the snow … it's too deep.'

Magnus gave her a kind smile. 'It's not so much far by the crow. I can take you if you really want.'

Julia shook her head. 'I think I'll stay for a couple more days. The snow will melt soon anyway.'

'Unless we have entered the ice age,' Magnus said.

Joseph was staring at her, a little smile on his lips. As he noticed her looking, he gave a little shake of his head and pulled off his backpack.

'We'd better get back soon,' he said, 'But we thought you might be hungry. We brought mince pies and a flask of coffee.'

'Unleaded,' Magnus said. 'But if you want the kick, I have some brandy warming in my inner pocket.'

Julia laughed. 'I'll be okay,' she said.

In the company of friends, the snowy road had lost its

threat. Julia took a deep breath of fresh air and smiled. Things would work out, one way or another. If you clung to the side of a train long enough, eventually you reached your destination.

'We should get back,' Magnus said. 'Soon, the sunset will come. Then, we will freeze.'

'It's about a mile,' Joseph said. 'It's not that far.'

Even so, it was almost dark by the time they returned, tired and cold, to Chapel Cottage. Mabel, sitting inside the window with Elizabeth, came running out, wrapping her arms around Julia.

'Dear child, whatever got into you?'

'I was trying to escape,' Julia said. 'I'm sorry. I just really wanted to see my family.'

'It won't be long,' Mabel said, as Elizabeth came out on to the front step behind her. 'Just hang in there a couple more days.'

'There you are,' Elizabeth said. 'Running off like that. What got into you? I thought my blood pressure would go through the roof.'

Julia opened her mouth to explain, then realised that conventional logic wouldn't work on Elizabeth, the way it worked on normal people.

'I'm sorry,' she sniffed, putting on an act that would have made her school drama teacher proud. 'I wanted to look my best for your wedding. I was trying to get back home in order to pick up my best dress and bring it back. And if I somehow didn't make it … that was the price I was willing to pay for your happiness.'

'Sisters!' Elizabeth gasped, throwing her hands up in the air and then dramatically pushed past Mabel to grab Julia in a bear hug. She smelled of expensive perfume which almost made Julia sneeze. 'You're the sister I never had. I can't believe you would sacrifice yourself for the happiness of me and my online fans. You're … wonderful.'

'Thanks,' Julia said.

'Well then,' Elizabeth said, pulling away and wrinkling her nose. She sniffed at the air, then sighed. 'Oh, the countryside.' Then taking Julia's cheeks in her hands, she said, 'Don't worry. I'm sure Julian's mother will have something you can wear. We'll get through this. I know we will.'

Before Julia could reply, Elizabeth had turned and swept back into the house. She clicked her fingers and then whistled. From the enclosure came the howl of a wolf, then Xavier came running up the path from the garden, his camera still in hand.

'I need you,' Elizabeth said, as Xavier followed her inside. Julia caught a glimpse of his camera screen and the image of a wolf before he went inside.

'It's grandmother,' Mabel said.

'And it's Joseph,' Joseph said.

Magnus frowned, then pulled up his sleeve and peered at a watch so complicated it looked like a robot attached to his arm.

'It is nearly five,' he said. 'I must do my security check of the village. It will take me into the vicinity of the pub, which might be open. I may have to go inside. For your safety, I suggest you follow.'

Joseph glanced at his grandmother, then at Julia, who shrugged.

'It's Christmas,' she said. 'Why not?'

HARD WORDS AND APOLOGIES

IT SEEMED like the entire village had a hangover from the previous night's karaoke, but Don had dusted off a pile of board games for the customers to use. Julia enjoyed beating Magnus, Joseph, and Colin—it was Kelly's turn for child duty back at the Grange, but according to Colin 'She was so rough this morning that she's only just back on solids'—which made Julia feel a little smug, even if Magnus was more interested in the pub's selection of brandies, and Joseph kept checking his watch and muttering about getting back to the wolves.

In the end, Magnus decided to stay for a nightcap with Colin, leaving Joseph and Julia to walk home. Even though Julia had drunk enough for a little Dutch courage, the first half of the journey was conducted in near silence. Perhaps it was the arduousness of trudging through ten centimetres of fluffy fresh snow on top of a crusty, lumpy under layer, but as the wine she had drunk started to make her dizzy, she finally plucked up the courage to say, 'I didn't get a chance to say congratulations.'

'What?'

'Your … ah … wedding. To Elizabeth?'

They walked on a few more steps in silence before Joseph said, 'Oh, that.'

'I mean, it must have been a whirlwind romance,' Julia said, her mouth running away with her. 'You met her two days ago. I never really believed in love at first sight, but when I saw you two together … I suppose it must be possible, mustn't it?'

Joseph stopped walking. Julia went on a couple of steps, then turned back. He was watching her, hands on hips, his face illuminated by a nearby streetlight. He somehow managed to look both bemused and disappointed at the same time.

'You are joking, aren't you?'

Julia frowned. 'About what?'

'About what you just said. About me and Elizabeth.'

'No. Why would I be joking? I mean, you're clearly hopelessly in love with each other.'

'I think you've drunk too much.'

Julia knew he was right, but admitting it would be admitting he was right. 'I only had a couple of glasses,' she said. 'Hardly a drop. I used to … be on my university's drinking team.' *Just shut up,* her brain was telling her, but she was like a snowball rolling downhill, picking up pace.

'In that case, it might be a good idea if you eased back a little,' Joseph said. 'I mean, once you hit your thirties, you'll start to age a lot quicker. Your body won't be able to keep up.'

'Once I hit my … I'm thirty-five.' *Had that been a compliment or not?*

'Well, it is pretty dark, and I'm five beers deep. Celebrating my upcoming marriage and all that.'

'I know it's not for real.'

Joseph let out a deflating sigh. 'Of course it's not for real. How could anyone marry her? She's not … human.'

'Finally we agree on something.' Julia stamped her foot, but it failed to have the desired effect. Instead of a hearty clump on road, she nearly tripped over on a lump of ice. 'So … why are you marrying her, then?'

'Not everyone gets married for love,' Joseph said, moving again, walking past her and on up the street, leaving her to catch up. 'It's business. You won't understand.'

'I watch plenty of art house movies,' Julia said. 'And I don't own a single Mills and Boon. I know what you're doing, even if you don't want to tell me.'

Joseph stopped again. 'Do you know why I was in Brentwell the other day?'

Julia wanted to say something sensible, but her mouth and brain were still refusing to align. 'Shopping for suits?' she snapped. 'You know, just in case some rich media starlet got marooned in your village and decided on a whim to marry you?'

Joseph sighed. 'Yeah,' he said. 'That's exactly right.'

He walked on, not waiting for her, his head lowered, and Julia felt like the world's biggest witch. She stood for a moment watching him, her mind yo-yoing between whether to apologise or whether to berate him further. Why not kick a man when he was down? By the time she decided that she could at least give him a chance to explain, it was too late. Joseph had turned a bend in the road and was out of sight.

Afraid of getting lost, Julia hurried to keep up, attempting to jog through the dark patch between the street light behind them and the next, almost hidden among snow-laden trees on the next corner. She needn't have worried, however, for as she reached it, the outside lights of Chapel Cottage appeared up ahead.

Of Joseph, though, there was no sign.

The snow had stopped again, and a full moon hung overhead. Julia walked up to the cottage, cleared a patch of snow off the low stone wall along the front of the garden and sat down. She looked up at the sky, briefly attempting to count the stars, before feeling rather ridiculous and giving up.

The moon was bright enough to illuminate the nearest hills. The lying snow reflecting the light made everything otherworldly, and Julia breathed it in, feeling so small yet so alive, like a caterpillar that had accidently hibernated and was only now beginning to transform. At the same time, she felt both happy and sad, at peace yet angry, filled with ideas yet content with where she stood in life. She tried to remember the last time she had felt so conflicted and failed, as though up to this point her life had been on a slow, downward slide she'd had no chance of arresting, even had she realised what was going on. For the first time perhaps in fifteen years she felt like she was grabbing the wheels of her own destiny.

She couldn't sleep, not yet. She thought about going for another—shorter—walk up the road, then changed her mind at the faint sound of a voice coming from around the side of the cottage.

The wolf enclosure. Julia walked down the path through snow-covered flowerbeds and out to the little shed. A light was on inside, and she heard Joseph's soothing voice coming from inside.

'Joseph?'

She gave the door a light tap, then stepped back, not wanting to alarm him. After a moment, it opened and

Joseph peered out, backed by a single dim bulb hanging from a cord in the ceiling.

'Julia?'

'I'm sorry. For what I said. I was just … drunk?'

She shrugged and smiled. Joseph looked at her a moment, then gave her a wide grin. 'Come in,' he said. 'There's plenty of room, and there's a little heater too.'

He stepped back for her to enter, Julia closing the door behind her. She found herself in a little standing space with a wire fence separating her from two brick-walled animal pens a few paces across. Small curtains hung across entrances in the opposite wall that led outside to the running enclosure. In the nearest, an empty dog basket lay in one corner, a bowl of water and an empty food bowl in another.

'Barry's outside doing wolf things,' Joseph said. 'But Bella's right here, nursing the pups. Come and take a look.'

He pulled up a low wooden stool, then adjusted a little paraffin heater so that Julia would feel the benefit of its heat. Then he pointed into the second pen. Bella, grey furred and majestic, lay on her side in the middle of another large dog basket, a cluster of small grey shapes that resembled sausages shuffling and shifting around her belly. The wolf was awake but looked exhausted. As her eyes regarded Julia, she gave a brief, tired howl as if in greeting.

'They're so small,' Julia said. 'Your grandmother said there were nine?'

'That's right. It's a pretty big litter. She's struggling a little, but I'm doing what I can to help out. Barry's being a bit of a nuisance so I'm keeping her gate closed for the moment, but once Bella's out of danger, we'll let him visit his little ones.'

'She's in danger?'

'She's a little weak, but she should be alright. If it gets too much, I might need to hand-rear a couple.'

'Can you do that?'

Joseph nodded. 'Put them on the bottle. The longer they stay with their mother, the better, though. I'm just out here to make sure there's no trouble and that she's eating and everything.'

Julia glanced over her shoulder and saw a camp bed folded up in a corner.

'Are you sleeping out here?'

He nodded. 'For the time being. It's convenient. Magnus snores louder than an avalanche anyway, and I let Xavier have my bed because perhaps his ears have gone beyond sound or whatever. For the first few days, I need to be with Bella, just in case there are any problems.'

Julia said nothing. The harsh way she had spoken to Joseph on the road was already haunting her, and she feared making it worse. In the end, all she could mutter was, 'Sorry.'

'What for?'

'You know, for what I said.'

'It's alright. My grandmother reacted pretty much the same when I told her. Pride doesn't pay bills though, does it?'

'So what were you doing in Brentwell?'

'I had to visit an estate agent about what to do about the farm. It's likely I'll need to sell off the land, but if I can, I want to keep my grandmother's cottage. She grew up here. I can't make her move somewhere else now. This is her home. The truth is, though, that we're sinking.'

'You can't afford to run it anymore?'

Joseph shook his head. 'We're in debt up to our eyes. No one wants real Christmas trees and the petting zoo was only ever a side project. Taxes and rates have gone up, and our income has gone down. I was hoping to get away with just selling off some of the land rather than the whole property.' He let out a little chuckle and shook his head. 'And then Elizabeth made me an offer. I thought she was joking at first.'

'About what?'

'Getting married. I thought she was making fun of me, but she wasn't. She was completely serious. Apparently she lives in a world I didn't even know existed, and some magical, fairytale Christmas wedding will send her popularity through the roof. And with popularity comes money. She offered me more than I can refuse, enough that I could hold off on a decision on the farm for another year.' He sighed. 'It might make me a laughing stock around here, but what am I supposed to do? I can't make my grandmother move to some retirement flat in Plymouth. I might as well dig a trench and throw her straight in. Getting married is a ridiculous idea, I know that. But only a fool would turn it down.'

'So you're going to do it?'

Joseph sighed. 'Yes. The day after tomorrow, whether I like it or not, I'm going to marry Elizabeth Trevellian.'

SAUNAS AND PICNICS

IT WAS another crisp and beautiful morning. Julia, who had left her curtains open, woke up to the sun streaming in across her bed. Outside, barely a wisp of cloud marked the sky, but the snow had obviously closed in overnight as the garden was once more a flawless blanket of white.

She took a shower before heading downstairs. It was a little after eight o'clock and she found Mabel alone in the kitchen.

'Ah, there you are, dear. I'm afraid the rest of them have already gone out. Well, except Joseph, who's still out with the wolves.'

'I can take something out to him if you like,' Julia said.

'Oh, would you, dear? That would be lovely. What are your plans for today?'

Julia smiled. 'My arms are killing me from digging all that snow yesterday, so I'm hoping I get something else on today's roster. Making paper chains, perhaps.'

'Well, it's good to see you looking so cheerful. And if you need to do a bit of a stretch out, you can borrow one of my Doreen workout DVDs if you like.'

'I'll probably be alright by the time I walk down to the village.'

'That's good. Just a day until the big event,' Mabel said. 'Well, events, plural, I suppose, if you count this ridiculous sham wedding.'

'I talked to Joseph last night,' Julia said. 'I understand why he's doing it.'

Mabel sighed. 'He's a good boy,' she said. 'His heart's in the right place. Even if his brain is bouncing down a road somewhere, about to crash into a brick wall. I don't know what he's thinking. We'll survive, somehow. We always do.'

Julia had something to eat, then took a tray of cornflakes and toast out to the wolf enclosure. Joseph was sitting where she had left him the night before, watching over Bella and her pups.

'Good morning,' he said, a little bleary-eyed. 'Is that for me?'

'For Bella,' Julia said, then at Joseph's crestfallen look, she smiled. 'Of course it's for you. I'll go back and get some coffee. You look like you need it.'

'I barely slept,' he said. 'One of the pups was struggling.' He leaned over the fence and pointed at a little one now sleeping beneath Bella's front paw. 'I had to keep pointing him in the right direction. I think he'll be okay now.'

'Bella looks tired,' Julia said, as the wolf, lying on her side, watched her. 'But she looks happy at the same time. Have you got names for them yet?'

'I don't want to get too attached to them, just in case. I'll wait a couple more days. What have you got planned for today?'

'I'm going to go down to the pub in a minute, find out what I've been assigned to do today.' She rolled her eyes.

'Probably clearing fallen trees or digging out blocked drains. Maybe climbing electrical poles to fix broken wires.'

Joseph laughed. 'Harry obviously thinks you're capable.'

'I was hoping for something easy.'

'Fixing the community centre's roof?'

Julia shrugged. 'Something like that.'

'I'm sure you could do it.'

'I can also make paper chains, and thanks to your grandmother, I know how to crimp a mince pie.'

'Cross your fingers,' Joseph said. 'If you like, once I've made sure all the little ones have drunk enough for the morning, I'll come down and help you.'

Julia looked at him. As their eyes met, she got a little lump in her throat, and for a moment couldn't bring herself to answer. She looked away, and when she looked back, she found he had also looked away, but then looked back at the same time too. They both smiled awkwardly.

'That would be great,' she said.

When she reached the pub half an hour later, the news going around was that the snowstorm had finally passed, and Birch Valley was set for a week or so of clear, warmer weather. Snow ploughs from Scotland had reached Devon, and were slowly clearing the roads around the village. By tomorrow, it was likely that the roads would be clear enough for traffic, and the first train was scheduled to depart from the station at 6.30 p.m. tomorrow evening, the 24th of December. Elizabeth and Joseph's wedding would be held at 11 a.m., with the village founding celebration now starting at two, brought forward in case any of the guests of honour wanted to make a hasty exit on the same day.

To her surprise, Julia's initial reaction was one of disappointment. By tomorrow evening her adventure would be at an end, she would be boarding a train with an onward ticket to Olive Hill, back to her family. Her brief sojourn in Birch Valley would be over, and the process of forgetting all about Joseph, the wolves, Elizabeth Trevellian, crazy lords in bedsheets, and the rest could begin.

Except she didn't want to forget about them. Even Elizabeth, she realised with a smile. To her surprise, on the day's roster she found herself in a group that just said, 'Meet at the Grange at 2 p.m.', with no other details given. It was not even eleven o'clock, so she decided to have a walk around the village beforehand.

Almost entirely encircled by hills, there wasn't far she could go before she came to snowdrifts blocking the narrow lanes heading out. Down by the train line, however, she found a path leading alongside which had been well trodden by dog walkers, leading through snow-covered fields with the river flowing gently alongside. The snow had melted enough that the river was no longer frozen, and to her surprise, Julia heard voices coming from a stand of trees up ahead. Cries of excitement were followed by laughter, the sound of feet running on wooden boards and then the splash of large objects hitting water. More screams and laughter.

Cautiously, Julia approached the trees, until she caught sight of a wooden shack standing on the edge of a pool perhaps twenty metres across. A boardwalk extended out from the shack's door over the water's edge. A group of people were sitting around, or splashing in the water. As she watched, the shack's door opened, someone came running out, and a moment later they jumped off the edge of the boardwalk and landed with a wild scream in the water.

'Julia!'

She had been about to run away, but Kelly had spotted her. 'Come and have a look at this! Is this not the best thing ever?'

Julia followed a path through the trees until she came out by the pool. Fed by the river, it was sandy-bottomed, just deep enough to swim in. Despite the snow, a couple of people were doing just that, sculling through the water, their breath puffing out in front of them. The shack was a little bigger than an average garden shed, and smoke was drifting languidly out of a chimney. Just behind it, a tall tree hung out over the pool, a tyre swing hanging from a protruding bough. A group of children in swimming costumes were taking turns to swing out and bomb into the water.

Kelly, in a swimming costume with a towel around her shoulders, came running over. 'Isn't this amazing?'

Julia stared at her. 'It's the middle of winter. What on earth are you doing?'

Kelly pointed at the shack. 'That's a sauna. It belongs to Lord Andrews. Go in there and warm up for a bit, then jump in the water. It's amazing. No one's had a heart attack yet.'

'I don't have a swimsuit.'

Kelly nodded. 'Come with me. None of us do. There's a communal box. Don't worry, they've been washed.'

Kelly led Julia over to the shack, where she retrieved a box and fished out a swimming costume. 'That's about your size, isn't it?'

'It's at least a couple of sizes too small!'

Kelly laughed. 'Nonsense. You're half my size. Come

on, there's a little changing room around the back, and Lord Andrews brought clean towels. I'll get you sorted, then we can divebomb together.'

Around the pool Julia recognised several people from the train as well as a couple of locals. Once she was changed, Kelly took her inside, and they sat together in the baking heat of the sauna, where Julia realised what she had thought was smoke rising out of the chimney was in fact steam coming from a water heater in the corner. The sauna, big enough to seat about fifteen people, was so hot she was sweating within moments.

'Isn't this great?' Kelly said. 'Apparently, it's imported from Finland. Bob said they have more saunas than people.'

'Bob?'

'Lord Andrews. We're on first name terms now.' Adopting a sudden posh accent, she added, 'Although it's officially Lord Robert Andrews, the Seventh Earl of Brentwater.'

'Brentwater?'

'The river's name.'

'He's the lord of a river?'

'Supposedly. Although he might have been having a laugh. Difficult to tell. He's quite obviously bonkers.'

'Is he here?'

'He was, but he's gone back up to the Grange to organise lunch. He drove us all down here on the back of a tractor and trailer. Honestly, I'll be sad to leave this place. We've never been able to afford a proper Christmas holiday for the kids. Fingers crossed it starts snowing again.'

Julia smiled. 'Alright. Shall we go divebomb, or what?'

'On three,' Kelly said. 'Don't think about it. Just run and jump.'

'Got it.'

'Three!'

Kelly was up and running, laughing as she took Julia's hand and pulled her along. They burst out of the sauna, almost knocking into two people just coming in, and ran across the wooden boardwalk. Julia stared with sudden horror at the pool of freezing water, aware it was surrounded by mounds of snow and still had patches of ice floating on its surface.

'Don't think about it!' Kelly screamed.

'It's all I can think about!' Julia screamed back, and then she was hitting the water, her whole body exploding with cold. She gasped as her feet touched the bottom and she stood up, the water coming up to her chest. Kelly was flapping about in the water nearby, and a couple of other people—including the family she remembered from the train—began to cheer. Then she was taking Kelly's hand and climbing back out of the water to sit, dripping and freezing on the side of the pool.

'How was it?' Kelly gasped.

'Cold.'

'You'll get used to it. Back into the sauna for five minutes, then we do it again.'

'Is it safe?'

'Who cares? It feels great.' Then, cupping her hands around her mouth, she shouted to Caitlin and Josh, who were splashing about at the pool's far end, throwing a ball back and forth. 'Don't get cold! Warm up every five minutes, please!'

They did a couple more brief swims, and then towelled off as the rumble of a tractor coming across the adjacent field indicated the arrival of lunch. Lord Andrews, dressed in a ridiculous checkered suit waved out of the window as he pulled the tractor and trailer to a stop in the snow. To

Julia's surprise, Magnus and Xavier were among a handful of people who climbed down from the trailer, then started unloading portable paraffin heaters and hampers of food.

'What happened to Elizabeth?' Julia asked as Magnus and Xavier climbed up a set of wooden steps on to the boardwalk, putting down a heavy plastic cooler which Magnus had obviously been carrying the bulk of. 'Is she here?'

'She's at the church, having the … how you say? Melt down,' Magnus said, expressing it as two clear words. 'I think we both lost the job.'

'Really?'

Xavier nodded. 'It might be temporary, depending on her mood and the availability of replacement staff. It wouldn't be the first time. She'll probably rehire us later with a small salary increase which will be her way of saying sorry.'

As Julia listened, she became aware of Kelly watching her. 'I thought you said he couldn't talk,' Kelly mouthed, loud enough to make Xavier smile, even as he pretended not to hear.

Julia was about to reply when Lord Andrews climbed up on to the boardwalk and clapped his hands together.

'Lunchtime, everyone!' he shouted, louder than was necessary and in a way that suggested he didn't spend much time around people. 'Eat your fill, as the heathen commoners might have you clearing snow again in the afternoon.'

'I think he's joking,' Kelly whispered. 'But you can never tell. He's a bit odd. I think it goes with the territory of living in a manor house all on your own. I imagine it would drive me crazy too.' Then, cupping her mouth again, she hollered, 'Colin! Can you get the kids out and dried?'

Everyone got involved, setting up the heaters around the boardwalk and laying down picnic mats before opening the boxes of food and sharing everything out. Julia could barely believe it as she found a cup of hot mulled wine thrust into her hands, and a plate piled with sliced turkey, roast potatoes that were still warm, stuffing balls, pigs in blankets, and even a massive Yorkshire pudding filled with gravy placed in front of her. She was still looking at it when a large platter of mince pies, sliced Christmas cake, and a whole, steaming Christmas pudding with a bowl of clotted cream beside it was put down in the middle of her group.

'Don't touch any of that until you've cleaned your plates,' Kelly told Josh and Caitlin, as the kids eyed up the dessert.

'This is a smorgasbord from the gods,' Magnus said.

Lord Andrews, mingling among the crowd, clapped him on the shoulder. 'Eat, my friend, eat! You think three potatoes taste good? Four tastes even better!'

'You have a good sense of the logic,' Magnus said. 'You are a man who knows the maths, no?'

Lord Andrews looked unsure how to respond, so instead turned to Julia. 'Ah, I hear you all are staying up at Chapel Cottage.'

'That's right.'

Lord Andrews tugged at the Christmas hat he was wearing, pushing a bouncing curl of grey hair back underneath. 'Ah. Tell me, how is dear Mabel?'

Julia glanced at Kelly, who lifted an eyebrow. When she looked back at Lord Andrews, he wasn't looking at her, but rather shifting from foot to foot like an uncomfortable child waiting for the toilet.

'She's fine,' Julia said.

Not looking up, Lord Andrews muttered, 'That's good. Dear of her.'

Then, as though regaining his composure, he muttered, 'Have a good meal!' rather louder than was necessary, then moved off across the crowd to talk to another group.

'Well, that was odd,' Kelly said.

'He hides the secret love,' Magnus said. 'He is the boy who cannot speak to the girl.'

'That describes most of them,' Kelly said. Then, standing up, she added, 'Right. Who's for another dip?'

14

CHANGING COLOURS

AFTER LUNCH and one more quick swim-sauna combo, Julia climbed onto Lord Andrews' trailer with the others for the ride up to the Grange. When they arrived, they found Harry Faulkner directing other groups of people in the construction of a stage at one side of the car park, and a huge pile of snow at the other. A tractor with a shovel attachment driven by Don dumped shovels of snow on to the top of a pile which a dozen people were then patting down and moving about until it resembled a lop-sided triangle.

'We need some bits of wood for the steps,' Harry was saying to a group of volunteers as the tractor stopped and the group climbed down from the trailer. 'Donald! Can you go down to the station and ask Stan if there are any unused railway sleepers lying around?'

From the cab of the tractor, Donald made a gesture that suggested Harry should do it himself.

'It'll melt by tomorrow anyway,' said Jim, the man Julia remembered from the train.

'But we can't have the kids slipping.'

'It's snow, that's what it's for.'

'Here's an idea for you,' Jim said, turning to point across the courtyard to a flagpole standing on a stone pedestal. How about we move it over there, to that flagpole. Then we can tie a rope to the top of the pole to help people pull themselves up.'

Harry nodded. 'You're a mastermind. Donald! We need to move the snow. Over there, by the flagpole.'

'Well, you'd better get your shovel then, because I'm on a coffee break for the next twenty minutes.'

Magnus jumped down from the trailer. 'You fools,' he said, picking up a shovel. 'You need to build the ice steps with the straw for the grip. Do you have the straw?'

Harry glanced at Lord Andrews, who just laughed. Another man standing nearby, came over, his shovel resting over his shoulder. 'We have some up at Clayfield Farm. Unfortunately, the drive's not been cleared yet so we'll have to carry it. How much do you need?'

'Martin, thanks,' Harry said. 'Is that alright?'

'No problem.

'Two bales should do,' Magnus said. 'I will come with you. I have the strength of two men, but if necessary, I will fashion a sledge from hand using two metal fence poles and a wood door.'

'The lad's got a sledge we could use. It's just Argos, but it should be strong enough.'

'Good.' Magnus glanced over his shoulder, then pulled a pair of sunglasses out of his jacket pocket and slid them on. With a smile, he said, 'I'll be back.'

As he headed off with Martin, Josh hissed 'Cool! Do you think he has an uzi?'

'I doubt it,' Kelly said. 'There's no way he'd get it through customs.'

They all got down from the trailer and followed Harry

over to a pile of shovels. Behind them, Lord Andrews announced via a loudspeaker that the house was now open for a giant game of hide-n-seek, which brought a cheer from a group of children in the midst of a snowball fight among the snowy shrubs of the Grange's front gardens.

'He's going to put on the sheet again,' Colin said, leaning close to Kelly and Julia. 'He can't resist. The man's nuts.'

'What are they building?' Julia asked, pointing at the giant pyramid of snow. 'Is it some kind of ice sculpture?'

Harry, standing nearby, laughed. 'It's a toboggan run,' he said. 'One of tomorrow's games. Five pounds entry. All proceeds go to charity.'

'Are you up for it?' Colin said to Kelly.

'Do you have a heavyweight class?' Kelly asked Harry.

Harry laughed. 'We can do. So far we've got primary kids, older kids, adults, and pairs. But get enough people and we can do anything.'

'I'll go with Magnus,' Xavier said suddenly from behind them. 'A certain win.'

Julia turned to him. 'Does that mean I have to go with Elizabeth?'

'Good luck getting her on that thing. Knowing her, she'll probably helicopter out as soon as the wedding is over.'

Julia looked around, wondering where Elizabeth might be. She would be lying to herself if she claimed she was worried about the media starlet, but Elizabeth had seemingly been everywhere, and now she was nowhere to be seen. And hadn't Xavier said she had suffered some kind of meltdown?'

'So, I thought you were like a cyborg or something,' Kelly—who had perhaps had a little something spicy in her drink at lunchtime—was saying to Xavier. 'Like perhaps you came from one of those 3D printers or something?'

'It's just a role,' Xavier said. 'Kind of like an elaborate school play. And please call me Xavier outside of Ms. Trevellian's earshot.'

'You're a robot?' Josh said. 'Like, do you have a secret compartment?'

'Only an inside jacket pocket or two,' Xavier said. 'For storing all my camera parts.'

Julia called back over her shoulder that she was going to watch the hide-n-seek for a while, since everyone was standing around, unsure what to do, but instead of going into the house, she headed out along the driveway, back towards the village.

Having had a pleasant morning so far, she hummed to herself as she walked, waving to a couple of families building snowmen in their back gardens, stopping briefly to chat with a woman she had met in the pub on karaoke night, and then pausing to throw a snowball at a couple of kids who bombarded her from behind a parked car. The sky was clear, the air crisp but not too cold, and the Christmas trees sparkling in windows, wreaths on front doors, and strings of lights over front garden bushes made Julia feel like she was walking through the picture on a Christmas card. When a robin briefly fluttered down from a tree, alighted on a bird feeder hanging in a garden nearby, and then chirped hurriedly at her before grabbing a seed and flying off, the feeling felt rubberstamped. Only when she saw the church tower rising through the trees up ahead did her buoyancy weaken a little.

Where was Elizabeth?

She went in through the gate and up the path to the porch. The main door was ajar, but apart from a pair of middle-aged women admiring the stained glass windows, the church was empty. Julia asked if they'd seen anyone else, but they told her no.

She headed back into the village, stopping in at the Deer and Grape to see if Elizabeth was perhaps inside, either drowning her sorrows or celebrating her imminent takeover of the village's celebration. However, neither the young man working the bar in Donald's absence, or Stan, the station master, enjoying a quiet pint in the corner while watching horse racing on a TV hung above the bar, had seen her.

Outside, she decided to head back to Chapel Cottage to see if Elizabeth was perhaps pressuring Mabel into baking a wedding cake. Halfway, there, though, she spotted Reginald and Edwina O'Fara, standing on a little bridge, peering down into the water gurgling beneath. Edwina appeared to be chanting something, with Reginald regularly checking his watch, then looking hopefully up at the sky as though praying for a fresh round of snow.

Julia had just decided to slip down a side street when Reginald spotted her and waved. Unable to escape, she approached them, Edwina's face turning grave as she looked up from the river and pushed a string of beads back from her eyes.

'Train girl,' Edwina said. Her head swayed from side to side like a hypnotic snake, her eyes seeming to revolve, an effect Julia realised was due to some rainbow-coloured contacts she was wearing that were reflecting the sunlight. 'Have your trials begun?'

Julia shook her head. 'Not that I know of.'

'You will face an uphill task, of that I am certain. But if you prevail, you will see beyond the curtain.'

'What curtain?'

'I don't know that yet, dear.'

'Right. Have you seen Elizabeth Trevellian?'

'The starlet with the smile, but the heart that takes a while?'

'A while to what?'

'To warm,' Edwina said.

'She dropped that bit to make it rhyme,' Reginald hissed, as Edwina gave him a sour look.

'You mean she's a bit of a snow queen? Yeah, that's her.'

'She is searching for something nice, to make her life more bright.'

'Okay, thanks. Which means?'

'She's in the flower shop,' Reginald said.

'The flower shop?'

'Over by the mill, where the waters run still.'

'Up that way.'

'Thanks.'

Julia hurried off before Edwina could give her any more prophesies. Up the side street, quaint terraced cottages closed in on either side, doors opening straight out on to the road. On the end was a little bakery, which she guessed was the mill Edwina had been talking about, then she saw a pond in an adjacent garden, its water frozen, and smiled. It was easy to see why Edwina O'Fara was such a hit on daytime weekday television.

And there, a couple of doors down, was a small flower shop with the French word Fleuriste above the window. Julia went inside, a bell tinkling. A little counter stood in front of her, a glass cabinet to one side, underserved with a limited selection of flowers. A few plastic flowers stood elsewhere in pots, along with a few dozen pot plants and a shelf of books on flower arranging and other florist-related topics. As Julia entered, an old woman came out from a back room, a worried expression on her face.

'Um, can I help you?'

'Yes. I'm looking for a … friend. I was told she was in here. Her name's Elizabeth. You can't miss her. She looks like she stepped out of a catalogue.'

The woman gave a relieved nod. 'She's back here, in the living room. I'm afraid she's in a bit of a state. Perhaps you can help?'

Julia just nodded. 'Sure.'

She went behind the counter, following the woman through a door into a quaint, cozy living room with beams across the low ceiling, and bookshelves cramped into nooks, ornaments and trinkets everywhere. Elizabeth sat on an armchair, hunched forward, a cup of tea clutched in her hands. On the seat of the armchair beside her was a basket of half-finished knitting.

Elizabeth neither acknowledged Julia nor moved in any way. The woman brought a chair from another room and set it down at an angle to Elizabeth's armchair so that Julia could sit down.

'She's been like that for twenty minutes,' the woman said. 'I think she's gone catatonic. By the way, my name's Dawn. This is my shop. She came in and asked for a thousand white roses for a wedding tomorrow. I told her I only had a dozen and six of those were plastic. She started jumping up and down, then a moment later she was crying on the floor. I wasn't sure what else to do with her. She wouldn't move so I literally rolled her onto a rug and dragged her back here. I got her to sit up and take a cup of tea, but she hasn't moved since. By the way, would you like tea, coffee, or hot chocolate?'

Julia smiled. 'Hot chocolate, please.'

'Marshmallows?'

'Sure. Thank you.'

'Just give me a minute.'

As Dawn went out into an adjacent kitchen, Julia

watched Elizabeth. Immaculately dressed as always, for once she looked fragile, her exoskeleton cracked, like a bug that had flown into a tree. Her eyes were damp with tears, and her hair, usually so perfectly arranged, had frizzed out, as though she had removed her hat, been caught in a sudden storm, and then forced her hat back on. The makeup below one eye was smudged, and her hands were trembling.

'Are you alright?' Julia said quietly. 'It's okay. Whatever happened, it's going to be okay.'

For a long time, Elizabeth didn't react. Julia reached out and gave her a gentle pat on the knee, checking her glove first to make sure it was clean, just in case Elizabeth's jeans cost more than her salary. Then, like a statue coming to life, Elizabeth slowly turned to face her.

'Do you think I'm shallow?'

'Ah....'

It was a question Julia would struggle to answer with any honesty, so she just shrugged. Then, with Elizabeth watching her, eyes demanding an answer, she muttered, 'I think we can all be shallow at times.'

'Yes, but if I was a swimming pool, and you dived into me, you'd crack your skull. Wouldn't you?'

'I ... ah ... think it's always unwise to dive into a swimming pool until you've checked it's safe.'

'If I was a puddle, and you wanted to jump into me, there'd be no splash, because there wouldn't be enough water, even though it was brown, and you couldn't see the bottom.'

Julia just shrugged again, wondering who it was easier to engage in conversation, Elizabeth or Edwina O'Fara.

'I was walking back from the church,' Elizabeth said. 'I was passing a shop window, and I looked inside at my reflection. I saw this beautiful girl staring back at me, but then I realised I could see through her, to the shop beyond, as though she wasn't really there.'

'That's pretty much the experience most people get when they look at their reflection in a shop window.'

'I know that, but … it was … metaphorical.'

'Right.'

The door opened and Dawn appeared, bringing two cups of hot chocolate on a tray, along with a plate laden with at least a full packet's worth of marshmallows. She set the tray down on a coffee table, then pulled it close to where the two women sat.

'Good to see you've woken up, dear,' she said to Elizabeth, then took the cup of tea out of Elizabeth's hand and replaced it with a hot chocolate. 'And I thought you might want a replacement. This one's gone cold, hasn't it?'

'Thank you,' Elizabeth muttered.

'And eat up,' Dawn said, giving the tray of marshmallows a nudge with her finger. 'I can't on account of my diabetes, but there's no reason two young lasses like yourselves can't indulge.'

'Thanks,' Julia said, as Dawn smiled and went back to the kitchen.

'So, you saw through yourself,' Julia said, afraid Elizabeth was going to freeze up again.

'Yes,' Elizabeth said, her voice ephemeral, like a breeze through an open window. 'And I realised … nothing mattered. None of it, not a single thing. My whole life has been a lie.'

'I wouldn't say that.'

'Oh, but it has. I can't remember the last time I did anything because I wanted to. Everything I do is to please other people. To improve my popularity, my ratings, my algorithms. But what for? What is it that's popular? It's not me. It's just a character.'

'Perhaps you ought to take yourself a little less seriously?' Julia suggested. 'Why don't you have a marshmallow?'

'I couldn't. My daily dieting tips, my Instagram dieting account has two million followers, I can't … I can't … I … *can.*'

'They're pretty good,' Julia said, stuffing two into her mouth at once. 'I tell you what. After we finish this entire plate, I'll take you for a walk up to the top of a hill so we can burn off all these calories.'

'But wouldn't it be easier to not eat them in the first place?'

Julia smiled, adding a third marshmallow to the mix. 'Easier, sure. But way less fun.'

Elizabeth gave a shy smile, then reached out and tentatively plucked a marshmallow off the plate with fake fingernails so long it wasn't even touching her fingers. She stared at it for a few seconds like some kind of alien artifact, them popped it into her mouth.

She chewed it, frowning. Then, with a sudden widening of her eyes, she turned to Julia and said, 'Wow, it's good!'

'You can't tell me that's the first one you've had in your life?'

Elizabeth shrugged. 'There might have been one when I was a child. I don't remember.' She took another. 'They're moreish, aren't they? Wow, I'm starting to feel a little dizzy.'

'Probably best not to eat too much sugar if you're not used to it,' Julia said, as Elizabeth stuffed a third marshmallow into her mouth. 'I'd take it easy.'

'I feel so free,' Elizabeth said. 'I've never felt free before.' Then, as abruptly as her mood had changed once, it changed again, and she covered her head with her hands and began to sob once more.

'Is everything alright?' Dawn said, leaning around the kitchen doorway.

Julia grimaced. 'Ah … I don't suppose you have any mince pies?'

15

CUTTING LOOSE

FEARING that in her newfound freedom, Elizabeth would eat through everything in Dawn's cupboards, Julia did the next best thing she could think of: she took Elizabeth for a pint.

Thanking Dawn for her hospitality, she led a swaying, disorientated Elizabeth back down the road to the pub, where they took a corner table near the log fire. Elizabeth claimed to have never drunk alcohol before, so to be on the safe side, Julia ordered her a pint of shandy with the emphasis on the lemonade, and a pint of local ale for herself.

'I feel like such a man,' Elizabeth said, staring at the size of the glass. 'It's huge.'

'Women drink pints too these days,' Julia pointed out. 'Well, a couple. More than that and you'll spend most of the night in the bathroom.'

'Are pub bathrooms safe?'

Julia laughed. 'It depends how much you've drunk and how low the ceilings are.'

'No, I meant the hidden cameras. The paparazzi.'

'We're in the middle of nowhere so you're probably good.'

'There's always someone trying to bring you down.'

Julia shrugged. 'Maybe in your world. In mine, most people don't care. They just get on with things.'

'It must be so nice.'

'But we don't get to stay in fancy hotels, ride in limousines, and wear coats that cost the same as an average car.'

Elizabeth stood up. 'It's just a coat,' she said, unbuttoning her coat and pulling it off, to reveal more expensive clothing hugging an enviable figure beneath. 'I imagine it'll burn just like a cheap one—'

'No!'

Julia jumped up and grabbed the coat just as Elizabeth attempted to throw it into the fire. 'Sure, it will,' she said, guiding Elizabeth back into her seat with one hand while holding the coat out of Elizabeth's reach with the other. 'Of course it'll burn, but why would you waste something like that?'

'I don't want it anymore. It's everything I hate about my life. Expensive, vacuous, extravagant—'

'And it looks pretty warm, too,' Julia said. 'Look, if you really want to do something useful with it, why not donate it to the village's charity auction tomorrow?'

'There's a charity auction?'

Kelly had mentioned that one might be a good idea as a throwaway comment over lunch, but there was nothing official. Julia had plucked the words out of nowhere, and it felt like a good idea. She had a couple of books in her suitcase she could submit. Perhaps she could have a word with Harry.

'Yes,' she said, confident the villagers would go for it. 'It's … to save the Christmas tree farm.'

'What a great idea,' Elizabeth said. 'They can have the limousine. And I have nine pairs of Prada shoes in a case. And there's my perfume, and—'

'You don't have to get rid of everything.'

'But I want to. I need to start over. Everything needs to change. I … hate myself.'

Elizabeth began to cry again. Julia patted her on the shoulder, as Don, now back working behind the bar, gave her a sympathetic smile. He pointed at the spirit optics and raised an eyebrow, but Julia mouthed, 'Best not to for now.' Then, to Elizabeth, she said, 'How can you hate yourself? If what you've said is true, that everything you do is for image, you probably don't even know yourself. Under all that … paint, and all those labels, you're probably quite nice.'

Elizabeth looked up, wiping her eyes. 'Do you think that's true?'

'Ah … let's see what we can find out. What's your favourite colour?'

Elizabeth frowned. 'Well, I ran a poll on Insta last year—'

'I don't care about the poll. What do you think?'

'Ah … green? No. White. No. Red? I don't know!'

'Okay, for now we'll just say you like rainbows. What about your favourite food?'

'Lettuce.'

'No, not the only thing you ever eat. What do you actually like?'

Elizabeth's face screwed up, and she looked utterly miserable. 'I once starred in a hamburger advert for TV, and it looked really nice.'

'You didn't eat it?'

'We used dummies on set. They were plastic. I had to bite down on it, and there was this detachable bit which came off, but on the advert they cut to some stock footage.'

Julia raised an arm, getting Don's attention. 'I don't suppose you do hamburgers, do you?'

Don grinned. 'We've got regular, double with cheese, spicy chicken, or the tractor burger.'

'What's in that?'

'Three burgers, cheese, bacon, relish, lettuce, gherkin, grilled aubergine, tomato, and a fried egg.'

'Sounds fantastic. We'll have two. Ah … why's it called a tractor burger?'

'Because it comes with a free sticker of a David Brown. Plus, you'd probably need one to pull it. Chips on the side? Or do you want a side salad? Lettuce, other green stuff?'

Fearing Elizabeth would take one look at a leaf of lettuce and climb back on the wagon, Julia shook her head. 'Chips will be perfect. With tons of vinegar.'

'Coming right up.'

As Don went through a door behind the bar, Elizabeth turned to Julia with a horrified expression on her face.

'What if I don't like it?'

'Don't worry. I imagine Magnus'll be along on in a minute. He'll see it as a light snack.'

'Magnus … I'm so horrible to him. And to X … although I don't think he understands human emotions.'

'I'm pretty sure he does.'

Elizabeth leaned forward, her eyes wide. 'He does? But he's not—'

'Human? I think he is.'

'Really? And I've been treating him like an abstract being all this time.' Elizabeth gripped her head. 'What's wrong with me? I feel like I just escaped from a cult.'

'Perhaps you did. The cult of social media.' Julia

smiled. 'Welcome back to the real world. It's nice to have you.'

Elizabeth frowned again, leaning forward. 'Do you think X has a real name?'

'Why don't you ask him?'

'How?' Elizabeth wailed, throwing her hands up in the air. 'There's no network connection here!'

Julia reached out and took Elizabeth's hands, pulling them down on to the table. She waited until Elizabeth had stopped hyperventilating, then looked into her eyes and said, 'Ask him with your voice.'

Elizabeth stared at her for a moment. Then, leaning forward as though about to impart some otherworldly secret, in barely a whisper she said, 'Do you think that will work?'

Half an hour later, during which time both Julia and Elizabeth had a decent go at eating their way through burgers designed for far bigger—or perhaps even multiple —people, the doors opened and a group came in, shaking off snow, their steamy breath fogging the glasses hanging over the bar. Among them were Magnus, Xavier, and Kelly's family. As Elizabeth jumped up and began to dizzily apologise to Magnus and Xavier for various misdemeanours, Julia went over to Harry and suggested the charity auction. With an excited grin, he told her they would squeeze it in during the afternoon, between the sledging competition and the group snowball fight.

Everyone seemed in good spirits, having apparently managed to complete the sledging hill and erect the stage to hold most of the events. Julia felt a little guilty for not helping more, but as Elizabeth jumped up and hollered,

'All drinks on my house!' to a series of confused cheers, no one seemed to mind. Don wheeled out the karaoke, and Harry put down a tray of freshly baked mince pies on the bar.

'What on earth happened to her?' Kelly said to Julia, as Elizabeth, hand in the air, practically begged for first go at the karaoke, dragging Xavier up to the stage behind her as though needing to prove he could actually speak.

'I think she's in the process of finding herself,' Julia said.

'More like humiliating herself.'

'It's Christmas. Isn't that what it's for?'

'I'll drink to that. What are we singing tonight?'

'I'm not sure.'

'Well, we can worry about that in a minute. I think you need to go and help her out.'

Elizabeth was waving frantically at Julia. As Julia eased her way through the crowd, Elizabeth leaned down from the stage and pulled her close.

'I don't know any songs,' she hissed into Julia's ear. 'Nothing longer than fifteen seconds, at any rate. What do I do?'

'There must be something. Didn't you listen to music when you were a child?'

Elizabeth's eyes widened. She gave a little hiccup, then muttered, 'Oh my. That beer's gone right to my head. Okay, I thought of one.'

She pushed away from Julia, swaying drunkenly, and said something to Don that Julia couldn't hear. As Julia headed back to Kelly's table, Don coughed into the microphone and said, 'Okay … first up, we have Elizabeth Trevellian and ah … X? And they're going to sing … ah … Happy Birthday.'

'It's my birthday!' screamed a voice from near the bar.

Julia turned to see Edwina O'Fara waving a glass of something pink into the air while Reginald sipped on a pint behind her.

'… ah … Happy Birthday to Mrs. O'Fara!'

'Miss! Miss!' Edwina shouted as people began to call out Happy Birthday. 'His name is Clutterbottom,' she said, pointing to Reginald, who gave a sheepish grin and shrugged. 'O'Fara is a stage name!'

Her protestations were drowned out by Elizabeth's singing. Holding the microphone far too close to her mouth, whatever tune she might have carried was lost as the volume rose and dipped, feedback squealed from the PA speaker and members of the crowd cried out for her to shut up, even as Edwina O'Fara swayed and clapped along. Xavier, for his part, stood nearby, looking nervous, as though waiting for the ordeal to end.

'At least that's something she's not good at,' Kelly said. 'What a racket. It's going to take some effort for us to top that. You want me to get in the schnapps?'

Julia grinned. 'It is Christmas, isn't it?'

They had a couple more drinks, then sang a couple of terrible renditions of classic Christmas songs, before Julia realised she ought to get back to Chapel Cottage. She had asked Don to call Mabel earlier and tell her that they had all eaten already, but it had been a long day and she was exhausted. Half an hour earlier, Magnus, Xavier, and Elizabeth had departed, the two men supporting the girl who seemed caught in a half-life between elation and misery, howling with laughter one minute, sobbing wildly the next.

'Can't handle her booze,' Colin said, then checked his watch and told Kelly they ought to be making a move too.

'That crazy fool was putting on a movie night for the

kids,' he said. 'I imagine about now he'll be getting the sheet out.'

'Do you want us to walk you back?' Kelly asked.

Julia shook her head. 'I'll be okay. It's not so far. And with all the Christmas lights, it's pretty bright now too.'

A few minutes later, still a little dizzy from the alcohol, she left, the cool night air on her face as she left the Deer and Grape a welcome relief after the stuffiness of the pub. It was a little after eight, and she did a circuit of the village before heading back towards the cottage, enjoying the snowy scenery, the lights strung up along most of the hedgerows, the Christmas trees glittering in living room windows and on front lawns. How everything seemed to have changed in just a couple of days. Birch Valley had felt like the end of the world when the train was forced to stop due to the snowstorm, yet now it felt like a magical, secret place, one where if she found herself trapped forever, she really wouldn't mind. There were definitely worse places to spend your time.

She had walked right to the outskirts of the little village, where a snowdrift marked the end of a road leading out. In the distance she saw lights, heard the hum of an engine, perhaps a snow plough making its way through. It wouldn't be long now. It had barely snowed all day and the warmer daytime temperatures had started melting off the standing snow. In a couple of days her adventure would be over, and she would be climbing aboard the train again to head back into the real world.

With a sigh, she turned and headed back through the village, but she hadn't gone far when she heard a familiar voice coming from around the corner of the next house.

'It must have clipped the edge, Mrs. Green. Don't worry, we'll put these back up where they were, and then tomorrow I'll come down with a bucket of cement and seal it up.'

Joseph.

Julia felt an uncharacteristic flutter of butterflies in her stomach. Convincing herself it was just from the drink—plus a little upset maybe caused by the tractor burger, which she had managed to eat more of than was probably safe—she took a deep breath and carried on, pausing at the turning into the side street beyond the house, where she found Joseph kneeling down beside a pile of rocks that had been knocked loose from a stone wall. An old woman stood beside him, stooped over, fluffy white hair covered by a Christmas hat as she leaned on a walking stick.

'Joseph?'

He looked up, and the spontaneous smile that appeared on his face made her stomach only flutter more.

'Julia! There you are. I was just taking a walk with Basil when I bumped into Mrs. Green here.'

Julia glanced around for the dog and spotted him tied to a gate post a little further up the street, sitting patiently. When he saw her looking, he gave a low, gruff bark. Julia smiled then took a couple of tentative steps forward. 'What happened?'

'I think a tractor must have backed into Mrs. Green's wall.'

'I can't let Felix out,' Mrs. Green said. 'My boy will escape.'

'Felix is Mrs. Green's Pekinese,' Joseph explained.

'He'll climb right over and go running off after cars or sheep or bicycles,' the old lady said, clearly distressed. 'I can't bear to lose him after I lost Daphne last year.'

'Daphne was Mrs. Green's cat,' Joseph pointed out. 'She ran off last summer.'

'Oh, I'm sorry to hear that,' Julia said.

'She came back,' Mrs. Green said. 'But those five hours she was missing … those were the longest five hours of my life.'

'Five hours? That's not so long for a cat.'

'Daphne only has three legs,' Joseph explained. 'She'd only gone a hundred yards up the street but she'd managed to get herself stuck in a storm drain by the river.'

'I thought I was going to die from worry,' Mrs. Green said. 'I couldn't bear it if it happened again.'

'We'll get your wall fixed,' Joseph said.

Julia rolled up her sleeves. 'I can help,' she said.

'It's alright—'

'No, I want to. I helped my dad build a stonewalled flowerbed once.'

'Oh, what a love you are,' Mrs. Green said. Further up the street, Basil barked, as though to agree.

For the next few minutes she helped Joseph replace the stones knocked free from the wall by the light of a nearby streetlight, as the stars glittered overhead, and Basil occasionally barked his encouragement. Joseph managed to convince Mrs. Green to go back inside, which she did for a couple of minutes, before returning with a fluffy, squat-nosed dog in her arms which she held out to watch the reparation progress.

'Nearly there, Felix,' she said. 'I know you need to do your business, but we can't have you getting out. You'll just have to hold it in for now.'

'That should do it,' Joseph said at last, standing up as he replaced the last stone. 'I'll be down in the morning with a bit of cement just to hold them in place. You should get back inside, before you catch a cold, Mrs. Green.'

'I'll just let Felix do his business,' Mrs. Green said, putting the dog down. Felix, delighted, scampered around in the snow before finding a suitable space in a corner to squat. Mrs. Green looked up at Joseph and Julia and smiled. 'Thank you both so much. You get along now. Do you live locally?'

'Ah, Mrs. Green, I'm Joseph from up at Chapel Cottage. Mabel's grandson. You play bridge together at the W.I.?'

'Ah, yes, that's right. Joseph. You've grown up so much. You were such a scrawny little boy. It's good to see you've filled out.'

'My grandmother's a good cook.'

'Yes, and so this must be your lady friend. I heard you were getting married. You make such a lovely couple.'

Julia froze. Joseph appeared to go pale beneath the streetlight.

'Ah, yes,' he said, giving Julia a brief glance.

'How lovely. I'm sure you'll have a long and happy life together. You seem so suited.'

Julia couldn't bring herself to look at either Joseph or Mrs. Green.

'Well … we'd best be … getting back,' Joseph stuttered.

'Nighty night,' Mrs. Green said, shuffling back inside. Felix gave a little goodnight bark, then scampered inside with her. The door closed with a soft thump, a key turning in the lock with a gentle click, and then Joseph and Julia were left alone in the silence, illuminated in the glow of the street light.

'Ah, sorry about that,' Joseph said. 'I wasn't sure what else to say.'

Julia could barely bring herself to speak. 'What … what do we do now?'

It was Basil that answered with a soft whump of a bark and a thump of his tail against the gate beside him.

'I think he wants to go home,' Joseph said.

16

SPILT HOT CHOCOLATE

THEY WALKED in silence for the first few minutes. Julia kept her head down, looking at her feet ostensibly to watch for pitfalls or patches of ice, but in reality because she still felt embarrassed and had no idea what to say.

'I'm sorry,' Joseph said again as Julia stopped to wait while Basil nosed in the hedgerow. 'It just kind of slipped out. Don't worry. Even if she shows up, she won't be able to tell, not with all the dresses and veils and things.'

'Just shut up.'

'I'm sorry.'

'And stop saying that.'

'Alright.'

They walked on again, but managed only a few steps before Basil found something else to nose at. A wind got up suddenly, showering them with ice from the branches of the nearest trees. Julia shrank away from it, and Joseph, hands in pockets but his coat unzipped, lifted one arm as though to shield her, even if his timing was off, the snow showering her regardless.

'Thanks,' she said, offering him a forgiving smile.

'You still have a bit on your nose,' he said, lifting a hand as though to knock it free, then thinking better of it.

'So, you're still thinking of going through with it?' Julia said, aware that someone had to take the initiative to move their conversation away from sorry or thanks. 'Marrying Elizabeth, I mean?'

Joseph shrugged. 'I suppose so.'

'I think she might be having cold feet.'

'Really?' He sounded more excited than perhaps was right for a man about to get married, but in the circumstances, it was probably understandable.

'That's what she told me. She might have just been having a moment, though.' Then, feeling as though the only way to stop herself from bursting into tears was to run her mouth, she said, 'Who knows? You might find you like each other. It might work out. What was it that woman said? You'll live a long and happy life together.'

'She was talking about me and you.'

'But you said she wouldn't know the difference.'

Joseph tugged on Basil's lead, pulling the dog out of a snowy hollow at the foot of the hedge. A large chunk of snow came away with the dog, and as he shook it off, it rained down on Joseph's boots.

'Ah, that sucks. Come on, let's just get home.'

'It's not my home,' Julia said before she could stop herself, aware it was the drink talking. Before she could even start to apologise, Joseph stopped, head lowered.

'And it won't be mine either unless I marry Elizabeth.'

'There's … there's the charity auction.'

'What charity auction?'

'I … I suggested it to Harry. People donate items and the proceeds go to saving the farm.'

Joseph stared at her. 'So the whole village knows that we're in trouble? I don't want charity—'

'So why are you marrying Elizabeth? Because that's exactly what this is.'

'Because … no one needs to know.'

Julia felt like a runaway train building up speed. She was on a roll, and there was no stopping her. 'So you expect them to think that some famous social media personality just shows up in this nowhere village, falls in love with a man like you so badly that she'll marry him after two days? Nothing suspicious about that, is there?'

'A man like me? What's that supposed to mean? Coming from a woman like you, who's what, thirty and single, and whose last boyfriend is in prison for burglary?'

'Car theft and fraud, technically.'

Joseph opened his mouth to reply, but Basil barked suddenly, derailing them both. Julia looked at the ground, while Joseph reached down and wiped a lump of snow off the dog's head.

'Look, I'm sorry,' Julia said.

'Me too.' Joseph smiled. 'Why don't we just go home— or back to Chapel Cottage, if you like—and drink some hot chocolate?'

Julia lifted an eyebrow. 'With a mince pie?'

Basil barked again.

'He can have a dog biscuit,' Joseph said, but as Basil whined and licked at his hand, he sighed. 'Or maybe just a bit of crust. A small bit.'

It was nearly ten o'clock when they got back to the house. Everyone else had gone to bed, but Mabel had left a plate of freshly made cakes and biscuits on the table with a note to eat as much as possible. Ordinarily Julia would have balked at the thought of so much sugar just before bed, but it was Christmas after all, so she went for a mince pie, a slice of maple syrup pie, and a cup of hot chocolate. Joseph chose the same, donating a piece of mince pie crust to Basil, who then retired contentedly to his basket.

'To be honest,' Joseph said, as they sat down facing each other on two armchairs, while the embers of a fire flickered in the grate, 'I'm not sure I can go through with it. Even if it does save the farm. It just doesn't feel … right. I've committed now, though, and I don't like to go back on my word. The church is ready, people are expecting … I mean, she'll probably annul it after New Year, when she finds something else to sell to her fans. They'll forget all about it. I mean, it won't even count as a proper divorce, will it?'

Julia gave a tired shrug. 'I have no idea. Would you want that hanging over your head, though?'

'You sound like you're trying to talk me out of it.'

'I'm not. It's your life. Your farm. I think it's quite an honourable thing to put your grandmother and your home before everything else.'

'Perhaps it's time to accept the inevitable. Nothing lasts forever, does it?'

'No, I suppose not.' *Although I wish this moment would last a little longer.* 'What am I thinking?' she said aloud, sitting up sharply in the chair, aware Joseph was staring at her.

'Are you alright?'

Julia shook her head. 'Sorry, I'm just tired. I drank too much earlier. I probably shouldn't be eating all these cakes either. Look, I think I'll turn in for the night.'

She stood up and walked across the room, acutely aware that it was the last thing she actually wanted to be doing, but that she was doing it anyway. As she sensed he might, Joseph got up to intercept her, but too quickly, knocking his hot chocolate to the floor. He let out a gasp as it hit the edge of a rug, fortunately not breaking, but spilling its contents across the stone slab on the floor in front of the fire.

'Ah, no.'

'I'll grab a cloth.'

'It's okay, don't worry—'

Julia tried to squeeze past just as Joseph turned, and his face was right there, inches from hers. There was an awkward pause as they looked into each other's eyes. Julia tried to breathe, but her throat felt tight, her heart fluttering.

'Julia—'

It didn't matter that it was just for show, for money, whatever. Joseph was getting married in two days. Julia forced her eyes away from his and hurried to the kitchen. When she returned a couple of minutes later, she found Joseph on his knees, soaking up the hot chocolate with a tissue he had found. He looked so adorably silly trying to soak up an entire cup's contents with one tissue that Julia couldn't help but laugh.

'No matter how many times you dip it, I don't think it can take any more,' she said.

Joseph looked up and smiled, the awkwardness that had passed between them apparently forgotten. 'But the ads on telly say they can soak up like a litre each.'

'Well, here's a cloth, just in case you need it.

'Thanks.'

She knelt beside him while he wiped up the hot chocolate, watching the way his hands moved back and forth with gentle, methodical strokes as though he took joy even from clearing up a mess. Her heart ached with both longing and regret, and in the end, she found herself standing up, backing away from him to the doorway.

'I'm going to turn in,' she said, her voice feeling hollow,

otherworldly, like another person speaking for her. 'I'll see you in the morning. It's the ... ah ... dress rehearsal, isn't it?'

Joseph looked up at her, but didn't smile. His eyes looked lost.

'Yes,' he said. 'It is.'

THE DRESS REHEARSAL

JULIA FELT MORE groggy than hungover when she woke up the next morning. She had forgotten to close her curtains, and now a warm, bright sun shone down on her bed. She got up, surprised to find it was only seven-thirty, and walked to the window.

The snow was beginning to melt, patches of green now visible in the field behind the house. The path dug through the garden was now an angular strip of grass between melting mounds of snow. Opening the window to let a cool breeze in, she heard engine sounds in the distance, snow ploughs and tractors clearing the roads.

In another day, her adventure would be over, and life would return to normal. Well, as normal as her chaotic relatives allowed. The sweet but sour days in Birch Valley and the people she had met would begin to fade into memory, however, and life would continue as it had before.

I don't want to go back.

The thought struck her with sudden, alarming clarity. She liked her life in Brentwell, didn't she? She had a flat—well, shoebox was a more accurate description—she had a job—chained to a desk—and she had friends … didn't she? She had work colleagues whom she sometimes shared a drink with after work on a Friday, and then there was Mary next door—currently looking after Mittens—with whom she had … once walked in the park? Or was it twice? Didn't they share a coffee once, too?

So, she didn't really have any friends, had a job she didn't like, and lived in a flat which was so small she could almost touch the opposite walls with her arms outstretched.

At least she had Mittens, her five-year-old cat, which she had found as a lonely, abandoned kitten in the car park outside. But then Mittens probably wasn't enjoying life in Brentwell all that much either. She took him down to the park from time to time, but she had no garden, and there wasn't even a decent view from her window.

Birch Valley seemed like a nice place, even though she had never imagined wanting to live somewhere barely a stone's throw from her own hometown. How would she ever afford to live somewhere like this, though? She didn't even want to think about possible house prices, and hadn't seen anything at all for rent while wandering around the streets.

Of course, she could do something drastic like marry the owner of a Christmas tree farm who kept wolves as pets and wrote poetry for a hobby … but then remembered with a daydream-busting POP that he was about to marry someone else, at a wedding for which she was the Maid of Honour.

She sighed and shook her head. A week ago, she couldn't have imagined any of this.

Downstairs, she found Magnus and Xavier tucking into French toast, Mabel humming to herself by the kitchen window while she waited for coffee to brew. Basil looked up from his basket and gave Julia a welcoming bark, but there was no sign of either Joseph or Elizabeth.

'Good morning,' Julia said.

'Ah, there you are, dear,' Mabel said. 'Coffee? I hear you got in late yesterday.'

'Sorry about that,' Julia said.

'Quite alright, dear.' She chuckled. 'When I was your age, I'd have been coming home as the sun was coming up.'

'Have you seen Joseph?'

'He's out with the wolves,' Mabel said. 'Sit down and have something to eat.'

As she pulled out a chair, Magnus looked up, a lump of French toast the size of Julia's fist hanging from the end of his fork. 'Are you ready for the dress rehearsal?'

Julia gave a reluctant nod. 'How's Elizabeth doing?'

'She went for the walk. This morning, her head is like the head of the bear.'

'She drank too much,' Xavier said with a shy smile. 'We got on the sherry when we got home.'

'Polished off a whole bottle between the four of us,' Mabel said with a chuckle. 'And then I taught her to barn dance.'

Julia raised an eyebrow. 'Seriously?'

'Docey-doe!' Magnus shouted suddenly, clapping his hands together, one knee coming up to bump the underside of the table.

'She's quite a pleasant young lady when you get to know her,' Mabel said. 'It's a shame she's lived her whole life inside a confectionary box. It's like when someone gives you a present which they had wrapped in a shop. It looks so nice that you don't want to open it and see what's inside, so you just leave it on the side, never really knowing what's in there.'

'This morning I will collect the car,' Magnus said. 'She wishes to be driven to the church.'

'I'm sure we can find some plastic flowers in the loft or some Christmas lights to decorate it,' Mabel said. 'It'll look lovely. Has she decided what to do about the dress?'

'She hasn't got a wedding dress?' Julia asked. 'I thought she brought a whole wardrobe with her.'

'She's asked local women to hunt out their old dresses and bring them to the church,' Xavier said. 'She'll pick the winner. The prize is that she'll wear their dress at the wedding, then they get to have afternoon tea and a shopping trip in London as Elizabeth's guest.'

'Lucky them,' Julia muttered.

'I tried to find mine,' Mabel said. 'But I think the mould had got to it. Plus, it would be far too loose for her. I was a bit plump in my youth. Liked the pork pies, I did. Only all this farm work that keeps the weight off. I'll tell you what, young lady. If you ever get married, pick a man who's not going to die on you.'

'I'll try,' Julia said. 'Although I don't think I'll ever get married. It's a bit late now. At least I get a decent view from up on the shelf.'

'You're still young,' Mabel said, patting her on the shoulder as she put a cup of coffee down in front of her.

'My mother married for the fourth time at eighty,' Magnus said. 'And he died after one year. She broke him in the bed.'

Mabel chuckled as Julia tried to hide herself behind a slice of toast. 'Oh, what a lucky thing. No better way to go out, is there?'

After breakfast, Magnus went and got the limousine from

where it had been buried in snow. It was quite a shock to Julia to see something the length of an average bus pulling up outside. When he opened the back door to allow her, Mabel, and Xavier to get in, she felt like she was jumping into a vacuum. It felt weird to step into a space where she expected to find seats, only to have to walk several steps past a table before she could sit down. And there was a door beside her, leading to another room at the very back.

'The bathroom,' Magnus said.

'You have a toilet?' Julia asked.

Magnus shook his head. 'That's through the door at the front. Back there is the bath.'

'An actual bath?'

'Yes. But now it is empty.'

'That's … too bad.'

'Ms. Trevellian liked to soak while on the road,' he said. 'I had to drive slow to stop the slosh of the water.'

'Isn't this exciting?' Mabel said. 'I feel like a queen.'

'Isn't Joseph going to come?' Julia asked.

Mabel's smile dropped. 'He said he would meet us there.'

A few minutes of careful driving later they pulled up outside the church. Magnus held the door for them, and they climbed out. The churchyard was still white, but some graves were starting to appear out of the mounds of snow, and the path had been cleared. Julia glanced up at the sky, feeling a little disappointed at the cloudless blue overhead. Another day, and she would be on her way back to her parents' house.

The vicar was waiting in the nave as they arrived.

'Good morning, Dennis,' Mabel greeted him cheerfully. 'Everything ready?'

The vicar gave a theatrical shrug. 'Depends what you call ready. Got more people inside than we'd usually have for anything bar Midnight Mass, yet we're still waiting on the main pair. They're not hiding in that monstrosity down there, are they? You know you're on a yellow line, don't you?'

'There is no sign of the line,' Magnus said.

'That's because it's under the snow.' The vicar sighed. 'Lucky the police can't get in. Although I hear they're looking at opening up the first road this afternoon.'

'And I was so enjoying all the new faces,' Mabel said. 'With a bit of luck we'll get another blizzard tonight.'

'I hope not,' the vicar said. 'Need to get out to the docs before they close tomorrow.'

'Ingrowing toenail again, Dennis?'

The vicar winced. 'Feels like someone jabbing a rusty nail in there with every step. I prayed for a bit of relief and all that, but Him upstairs isn't listening.'

'I imagine he's busy with Christmas,' Mabel said. 'Shall we all go in and see what's going on?'

They headed inside. Half a dozen women had shown up with wedding dresses in boxes and were standing around at the back, looking uncomfortable. A handful of spectators had also come—Julia gave Kelly a wave, while Edwina O'Fara glared at her from the back row and did something weird with her hands.

The vicar sighed. 'We were supposed to start ten minutes ago. Should we call it off?'

'Give them a minute or two more, Mabel said. 'I imagine they're both just delayed.'

'You're the Maid of Honour?' Dennis said to Julia.

'Ah, yes.'

'And you're the best man?'

Xavier nodded.

'And I'm the father of the bride,' Magnus said with a proud grin.

'Well, I suppose we could run through a few things. Where people stand and all that. We'll need some stand ins.'

'I will be the man, you the woman,' Magnus said to Xavier.

'Why me?'

'You think I can get on those dresses? They will tear like I am the Hulk.'

'Why can't Julia wear the dress?'

'I'm the Maid of Honour!' Julia said, stepping back. *And what if Joseph shows up while I'm standing there in a wedding dress? And worse, what if Elizabeth then shows up?*

'I could be the father of the bride,' Mabel said. 'Isn't this exciting? It's like roleplay. I haven't done that since—'

The church door flew open and a man with wild curly hair burst in. Dressed in a dinner suit that quite literally had spiderwebs hanging from its sleeves, he carried a huge box over his shoulder.

'Bob, what are you doing here?' Mabel said.

Lord Andrews looked up. 'I made it, thank goodness.' He set the box down on the floor. 'At last, the time has come for this to be worn.'

He lifted the lid to reveal an ornate, elaborate wedding dress, still wrapped in its original packaging. It looked unused, if somewhat old.

Mabel put up her hands over her cheeks. 'No, Bob, not now, please.'

'I just saw a young lady in tears,' Lord Andrews said. 'Drowning her sorrows in a pub. And then, I saw a young man, his face ashen, chasing a wolf across a field. Two lovers … parted. A wedding … unfulfilled. I am here, Mabel, my dear. I am here … for a second try.'

'Does he know this is just a dress rehearsal?' Julia whispered to Magnus.

'The fool has lost his mind,' Magnus said.

Lord Andrews clearly wasn't done. He pushed the dress aside and got down on one creaky knee, wincing and clutching at his back, then pulled a little box from his pocket. Wiping away a coating of dust, he lifted the lid to reveal a diamond ring that left Julia staring and Xavier reaching for his camera.

'Mabel Swann, the unrequited love of my life … fifty years after you turned me down and broke my fragile heart, will you marry me?'

Xavier was frantically taking pictures. Edwina O'Fara appeared to be attempting to levitate. Kelly was cheering, while Magnus was watching the scene with an amused grin. Julia looked from the old suitor to his potential bride, wondering if the day could get any weirder, while at the same time hoping Mabel would say yes.

Then, just as it became so silent in the church you could have heard a snowflake landing, a bell thundered overhead, making Julia cry out in shock and clutch her chest for fear of having a heart attack. She spun around, and when she looked back, Mabel was hurrying out of the church, leaving Lord Andrews where he knelt, the ring still held out, his face crestfallen.

'I think it might be better if we call time on this for now,' Dennis said. 'Is anyone up for nipping down to the pub for a quick lunchtime pint?'

18

TIME FOR TEA

MAGNUS OFFERED to give everyone a lift down to the pub in the limousine. When they found Mabel outside, however, the old woman declined, and Julia, with still the last nibble of a hangover, decided to walk her back to the cottage instead.

'I … ah … guess there was a little history there?' Julia said, catching up with Mabel, who was walking remarkably fast for a woman of her years, even if the road itself had been cleared of snow.

'Oh, my dear, I can't start getting involved with past flames at my age,' Mabel said. 'And Bob, he's not exactly marriage material, is he?'

'He's … rich?'

'Of course he is, dear. But there's more to happiness than money. Look at the little meltdown that caused the whole debacle. Neither of the big pair showed up, did they? Goes to show it was a silly idea from the start, wasn't it?'

'I suppose we should go and find them.'

'They're both adults, they'll be fine for a while,' Mabel

said. 'Let's have a cup of tea and a mince pie, and then I'll tell you all about Lord Bob Andrews.'

Julia helped Mabel tidy up and prepare the tea things, then carried the tray for her into the little living room, arranging it on the coffee table as Mabel sat down.

'Please, dear, tuck in.'

Julia had eaten enough mince pies to last a lifetime, but there was always room for one more. 'These taste so good,' she said, taking a little bite. 'I've never tasted any as good as this.'

'It's all in the fruit,' Mabel said. 'Dry it for a couple of years, then marinate it in a bit of port before putting it into the mix. Gives it that little extra sweetness.'

'How much would I need to eat before they got me drunk?'

Mabel grinned. 'Four or five. Lucky there's not much driving to be done.'

As they sipped their tea, Julia said, 'You must be looking forward to getting rid of us. I heard the roads should be open today, and the ice all cleared by tomorrow.'

Mabel shook her head. 'Not for a moment. I told you this used to be a B&B, didn't I? It's been lovely having people around again. I suppose, in a perfect world, Joseph would marry and have a family, and they would all live here, but having a few visitors is a decent replacement. We're social animals, us humans. We're not meant to live in isolation.' She chuckled. 'I've even grown fond of Elizabeth. She takes a bit more getting used to than most, but there's definitely a human being in there.'

'Perhaps ... perhaps she could marry Joseph after all.'

Mabel chuckled again. 'No chance of that. They're too different. He needs a more down to earth girl. Someone like—'

—please don't say it—

'—that T.V. presenter. What's her name? I think she used to do Blue Peter back in the eighties.'

Julia gave a nervous laugh. 'I'm sorry, I don't remember. I was busy being born in the eighties, although I missed most of it.'

'Anyway, he needs a nice girl.' She leaned forward, lowered her glasses a little, and peered at Julia, eyes narrowing. 'You don't have plans for tomorrow morning, do you?'

Julia's face burned. 'Ah … I'm supposed to be the Maid of Honour.'

'Ah, it's only a couple of steps to the side and a few more words. Then I could show you how to make my mince pies.'

Julia really wanted to go out and look for Elizabeth, or jump into a freezing lake, or pretty much anything other than be interviewed for the vacant position of Joseph's wife, but she was stuck, so she decided to change the subject.

'You were going to tell me about Lord Andrews?'

'Ah, yes.'

Mabel got up and shuffled over to a sideboard. She squatted down, slid open a cupboard door, then withdrew a thick photograph album. She made room on the coffee table then opened it and began to flick through heavy pages, the plastic covers creaking over ancient black and white photographs.

'Here we are.'

She pointed at a black and white school photograph. Julia marvelled at how smart the children looked, the boys in button up shirts and ties, the girls in knee-length frocks.

'Can you spot young Bob?'

Julia frowned, trying to guess which of these little kids was now an elderly man who liked to run around in a bedsheet. They were all in orderly lines, staring dead ahead, except—

'This one?'

'Bingo.' Mabel shook her head and gave a nostalgic sigh. 'Any other kid would have got the cane for sticking their tongue out in the school photograph, but the Andrews family funded the school's new gymnasium that year. Of course, it's all long gone now. Not enough kids left around here to keep it open.'

Julia stared at the slightly blurred image of a little boy holding up his hands to his ears and sticking out his tongue at the camera. 'So, he was the class joker?'

'Completely. The butt of all the jokes, although he was never properly bullied because of who his family was. At that time, most of the land round here was owned by the Andrews family. It might have got worse in secondary school, but he went off to some private school up in London, then to university, then he got some job overseas in the foreign office that his dad probably set up. He'd only appear for a few days here and there, every year or so.'

'And he asked you to marry him?'

Mabel sat back in her chair and smiled. 'Yes. A couple of times, actually. We had a bit of a fling once, on one of his jaunts home. Just a bit of fun, and there wasn't really anything to it. I thought he was joking the first time around, and by the second I'd got married. He disappeared for a few more years, then after his parents both died, he came back to rule, so to speak. It's not all that special, though. His family sold most of the house off to the National Trust thirty odd years ago. He only lives in one small wing.'

'Really? I thought—'

Mabel shook her head. 'No, no. He still thinks he owns it, but he doesn't. Knowing Bob, though, he'll be loving that all the staff are blocked out. He's probably taken down all the signs and is proper lording it up there. I mean, he's better off than we are, but not by a great deal.'

'That's sad.'

'Is it? What makes you happy, dear? Money?'

Julia frowned, then shook her head. 'I don't know. I don't really have enough of it to know. My cat makes me happy. My family, even the crazy ones. Meeting new people.' She smiled. 'Jumping into freezing cold rivers.'

'And there you have it. Another mince pie?'

'Sure, why not?'

They ended up eating another two each, then Mabel drifted off to sleep in her chair. Julia cleared up, draped a blanket over her, then went out for a walk.

She found Joseph where she had expected, up in the wolf enclosure, watching the pups. Already slightly bigger, they bullied at Bella's teats as their mother lay watching them.

'There you are.'

Joseph looked up and gave a nervous smile. 'Hi.'

'We were waiting for you.'

He looked like a dog about to beg for food. 'Elizabeth?'

'No, she didn't show up either.'

Joseph let out a sigh. 'I knew it was a bad idea. At least she figured it out too.'

'Even so, a lot of people were put out. Even if we did almost see Magnus in a dress, and then Lord Andrews proposed to your grandmother.'

'Really? Again?'

'You know about that?'

'He proposes practically every time he sees her. She was considered a bit of a catch in her younger days, I remember Dad once saying.'

'Has Lord Andrews never married?'

Joseph shook his head. 'Nope. He's lived up there on his own for years.'

'That's too bad. I feel a little sorry for him really.'

'He's doing okay. He's a sandwich short of a picnic, that's for sure.'

'So the marriage is officially off?'

Joseph sighed. 'It looks like it. I suppose I'll have to apologise to Dennis and practically half the village, even though it was never my idea in the first place. All I wanted to do was keep an eye on these guys.'

'And how are they?'

'The little one, he was struggling in the night. He couldn't get to a teat on his own, so I had to keep nudging him. He's starting to build his strength now. As long as I keep checking up on them, they should all be okay.'

'That's good news.'

Joseph looked up again. 'I imagine in the world of delayed trains, ceremonies, and celebrity weddings, it's of little consequence, but it means a lot to me. It's the small things, isn't it?'

Julia stared at him for a moment longer, then sat down on the bench beside him. She felt comforted just by his presence, even if there was a twinge of something else less pleasant—was it jealousy?

'What are you going to call them?' she said at last.

Joseph smiled, for the first time looking genuinely happy. 'I called Harry this morning,' he said. 'I told him I'd heard about the supposed charity auction, and thanked him for his efforts. I said I'd like to auction the chance to name eight of the wolf pups, but only on the condition that all the proceeds from the naming auction go to the children's home in Brentwell.'

'That's kind of you. Are you sure?'

'We'll survive,' he said. 'This business with Elizabeth …

it made me realise all the things I don't want to do. You can call it pride if you like, but there are more deserving people than us. I can sell off a field or two, that will keep us afloat for a while. And maybe we can work on expanding the petting zoo a little. These little guys will certainly bring in the kids for a while.'

Julia watched him. The way he talked with such passion about such selfless things made her heart lurch a little. It made her angry at herself to think it, but she wished he would talk about her that way. She looked at the wolf pups, so small and innocent, nuzzling against their mother. One, two, three, four, five, six, seven, eight—

'Hang on a minute,' she said. 'You said you were auctioning the naming of eight of them. But there are nine.'

Joseph smiled. 'I know. This little guy,' he said, pointing to the smallest. 'I want you to name him.'

'Me?'

'Yes.'

'Why me?'

He took a deep breath. 'Because, Julia … with all the crazy things that have happened over the last few days … everything began when I … when I saw you on the train.'

Julia's cheeks and neck were burning. She wished she had a decent excuse to make him turn the heater off.

'You saw me….'

'Yes. And I figured that after I got off the train I'd go back to the farm and carry on, and I'd never see you again, but … you got off the train. And then you ended up staying at the cottage. And it … it was all a bit overwhelming.'

'I don't understand.'

'I don't want to get married tomorrow,' Joseph said. 'I

really don't. But … before you leave, I hope perhaps we can … I don't know, take another walk together?'

Julia's heart was thundering so hard she couldn't bring herself to speak. She swallowed down a lump in her throat the size of an apple, and was about to force out some grunt of a reply, when the door to the shed flew open, to reveal Magnus standing there. Appearing so huge he could have lifted the shed and flung it like a caber, he leaned down and said, 'Have you seen Elizabeth? We looked everywhere. She has gone.'

19

AN UNEXPECTED SURPRISE

'NO ONE HAS SEEN her all of the day,' Magnus said, as Julia and Joseph followed him out to the limousine, which was parked in front of the house. 'It will soon be dark. She lacks the skills for survival in the wilderness.'

Xavier was waiting by the car. He held up his phone as they approached. 'She answered the phone,' he said, 'So we know she's alive. However, when I told her it was me, she said, "You don't exist!" and hung up. I should have pretended to be Magnus, but I couldn't pull off the voice.'

'Did she give any indication as to her location?' Magnus said.

'None.'

'We will have to track her.' Magnus lifted a bottle of perfume out of his jacket pocket. 'I have the scent.'

'Can't we just follow the tracks like you did when I ran off?' Julia said.

'Most of the roads are now clear of the snow,' Magnus said. 'Tracking you was like stalking a wounded deer. A practice.'

'I'll try harder next time,' Julia said with a smile.

'I'll get Barry,' Joseph said, running back up the path. Turning to call over his shoulder, he added, 'He's a little temperamental, but he knows how to track.'

'Dark will fall at sixteen hundred hours,' Magnus said.

'You mean four o'clock?' Xavier asked.

'Yes. Your camera. Does it have a heat sensor?'

'I think so.'

'We will use it. She may have taken cover to hide from imaginary drones.'

Joseph came jogging back down the path, with Barry straining at the lead in one hand, Basil in the other.

'Your other beast can track too?'

Joseph shook his head. 'No, but he hasn't been out for his walk yet. Two birds with one stone, and all that.'

'Let's go.'

Joseph took the perfume bottle from Magnus then squatted down and held it up in front of Barry. He pressed the stopper and the dog leaned forwards to take a little sniff, then whined and shrank back.

'Doesn't look like he's a fan,' Julia said.

Barry did a couple of circles in the road, Joseph feeding out the lead to give him room. He sniffed at the tarmac, then lifted his head, let out a little whine, and darted off towards the village.

'I think he's got it,' Joseph said, hurrying after the dog, then finding himself nearly split in half as Basil decided to go in a completely opposite direction.

'I'll take him,' Julia said, taking the otterhound's lead from a relieved Joseph, and tried to pull him after her, as he found something interesting in the icy snow by the roadside and began to dig with such ferocity that he showered Magnus and Xavier with clods of sleet.

Barry had already started off down the road, dragging Joseph after him. Basil noticed the wolf's departure and bounded in pursuit, dragging Julia along behind.

The footpath led them down into the village's quaint centre, up to the door of a little confectionary shop which was now closed. After nosing around a little, they picked it up again, following it as it led down past the pub to a pretty humpbacked bridge over the river, where Elizabeth had apparently paused for a while to contemplate life. Then, the footpath led back the way they had come, then up the gentle hill through the village's few residential streets in the direction of the Grange.

'Perhaps she decided to upgrade to someone a little older and richer,' Joseph said, as Barry briefly paused at the start of the wide driveway before heading inside.

'Oh, where have they gone? Magnus and Xavier were right behind us, but they seem to have disappeared.'

The road behind them, the surface cleared of snow which was still piled along the verges, was empty.

'Perhaps they got lost,' Joseph said. 'Let's just look up here and see if we can find her, then we'll double back.'

The driveway up to the Grange was like something out of another way of life. Wider than any of the roads through the village, it was lined by snow-covered pines which hid any view of the country house itself, which was located around a wide arc in a hollow near to the river flowing down the valley and through the village.

'Was this the kind of walk you were thinking about?' Julia said, as Barry and Basil briefly converged, distracting each other long enough to engage in a brief playfight.

'Perhaps without the dogs,' Joseph said, holding her gaze for a long moment before Barry broke into a sudden dash, jerking him away. 'Something a little more … peaceful!'

With patches of ice still covering areas of the driveway,

he had no choice but to follow or risk being pulled off his feet. Basil, thankfully, probably beginning to tire, followed at a more leisurely pace as the driveway arced around a corner and dipped downhill, the Grange coming into view.

Now that she knew Lord Andrews's secret, the signs were easy to spot. Signposts with the National Trust logo indicated the various themed walks through the garden— the Riverside Way, the Lilac Garden, the Rose Field—and there was even a small, glass-framed visitor centre tacked on to the right side of the house, now with a CLOSED sign hanging in the window.

The courtyard, set up for tomorrow's festivities, appeared at first to be empty, then the sound of faint voices came from behind the towering Christmas tree set up in the centre. Most of the snow had been cleared, but there were marks in the gravel to indicate that a person had come this way.

'I think we've found her,' Julia said, as they came around the angle of the Christmas tree. 'I think … oh.'

Joseph stopped suddenly, Julia bumping into him.

'Grandma?'

Instead of Elizabeth, as they had expected, Mabel stood there, held gently in the arms of Lord Andrews, a wide, beaming smile on his face, his wild curly hair pressing out from beneath a Christmas hat. Mabel had removed one glove, and a glittering diamond ring shone on one finger.

'Grandma? What's going on?'

The pair of them giggled like school children. Mabel smiled. 'I had a bit of a change of heart, didn't I? I figured both me and Bob are getting a bit long in the tooth, so why not give it a try?'

Julia glanced at Joseph, who was staring, mouth agape, at the couple as the sun suddenly dipped beneath the horizon and the solar powered Christmas lights on the tree came on, bathing them in cool reds, greens, and yellows.

'But … we were following Elizabeth. We were tracking her perfume.'

Mabel blushed. 'Oh, really? I wondered why you'd brought these two out. I just thought I ought to tart myself up a bit for the occasion.'

20

TAKING THE PLUNGE

'I NEED A DRINK,' Joseph said, as they headed back to Chapel Cottage after leaving Mabel and Lord Andrews to hastily finalise details for their wedding tomorrow morning. Julia had retained her place as Maid of Honour, with Joseph added as an usher, alongside Magnus and Xavier. Lord Andrews, apparently, had decided to ask both Harry and Donald to share best man duties, in the interest of building better social relations with the rest of the village. Elizabeth, if they could find her, would now be another bridesmaid.

'I'm sure I can make up a hot chocolate,' Julia said. Then, with a smirk, added, 'If you promise not to spill it.'

'I'll try,' Joseph said. 'But my hands are still shaking. That wasn't what I was expecting to find.'

'Me neither,' Julia said. 'Especially after we talked about it. But I suppose that's Christmas, isn't it? It does funny things to you.'

They checked on the wolf pups, put Barry back into his enclosure, and then let Basil into the house.

'Are you still looking forward to leaving tomorrow?'

Joseph said, as they walked back out of the gate and headed down the hill towards the village. 'I mean, you must be excited about seeing your family again.'

Julia shrugged. 'Yes, and no, I suppose. They're my family and they're great, but they're a bit crazy, and I'm really quite enjoying my time here. It's like a weird, magical dream.'

Joseph stopped. 'Why don't you ask them to visit here?' he said. 'The roads should be open in the morning, and there's plenty of room at the cottage. Plus, didn't you say they have a camper van? They could park it in the driveway.'

'My uncle does, yes. Are you sure? My cousins are a bit … odd.'

'They should fit in perfectly in that case,' Joseph said. 'I'm starting to think that you're the only normal person I've met in the last few days.'

Joseph was close to her again, close enough that he could have reached out and taken her hand. It was getting dark, the gloom taking the edge out of the day, making the harder questions easier. As a breeze got up, Julia surreptitiously swung her gloves, then brought them to rest, one glove gently resting against Joseph's. Her heart was thundering, her throat dry.

'Is that a good thing or a bad thing?' she said, wondering whether she sounded husky and romantic or just dehydrated.

'A good thing,' Joseph said, taking the bait and closing his fingers over hers.

'That's good,' Julia said, feeling like a bad actress in a daytime soap opera.

His lips brushed hers. Julia closed her eyes, waiting for the full kiss, wondering how it would feel, whether his lips would be warm and soft or cold and chapped.

'Ah, there you are!' came a loud, powerful voice. 'We went to the pub but we did not see her.'

Julia opened her eyes and smiled, Joseph's face blurry in front of hers. They touched foreheads gently then reluctantly pulled away.

Magnus was striding up the road towards them, Xavier hurrying to keep up.

'We checked the forest with the infra-red,' Magnus said. 'Did your trail go cold?'

'I'm afraid so,' Julia said. 'Mabel had ah … borrowed Elizabeth's perfume.'

'Elizabeth's phone is still ringing, but she's no longer picking up,' Xavier said. 'Do you think she could have been abducted, or eaten by a bear?'

'Unlikely,' Joseph said. 'But I suppose we shouldn't rule anything out. We can take Barry out again in the morning, but I think he was a little worn out.'

'We need to think outside of the box,' Magnus said.

'You said you went to the pub?' Julia said. 'Who was there?'

'Some local people,' Magnus said. 'And the crazy woman.'

'The mystic? Edwina O'Fara?'

'Yes. She told the fortunes to the gullible fools.'

Julia remembered what Edwina had told her. *Your time will come, dear. But not without trial, I fear.* Then, later, near the flower shop: *You will face an uphill task, of that I am certain. But if you prevail, you will see beyond the curtain,* and finally, *the bells of a church will leave your heart in a lurch, but if you bide your time, what you want … you will find.* It was the kind of freely interpretable mumbo-jumbo that she could tell anyone, but Julia—who didn't so much as believe in luck or fortune enough to buy a Lottery ticket—supposed it could mean something, if she wanted it to. And it was Christmas, after all. Time to suspend belief.

'Let's ask her,' Julia said. 'She might be able to tell us where Elizabeth is.'

'Worth a try,' Joseph said.

As a group, they headed back down to the pub. It was buzzing with people, all filled with Christmas cheer. Trays of mince pies lined the bar, and someone had donated a huge Christmas cake which had been hacked into monstrous slices. Behind a group of teenagers in Christmas hats playing a game of pool, Edwina O'Fara sat at a table with Reginald beside her, a pack of cards spread out in front of her. Kelly's husband, Colin, currently sat opposite her, a frown on his face.

'So that one there means that next year I might get wealthy, but that one there means that I might not?'

Edwina O'Fara gave a sage nod. 'Yes, yes. Your interpretation is correct.'

'And this one means there's going to be love in my life?'

'Yes, yes.'

'Well, I suppose it is our fifteen-year anniversary next year.'

'The cards don't lie,' Edwina said, her voice, soothing, like this hiss of a snake. She turned over one more. 'Ah, yes, something good will happen. Do you have any special plans?'

Colin scratched at his ear. 'Um … ah, yes! We're going to Portugal for a fortnight over the Easter holidays.'

'Of course you are,' Edwina said. 'The cards told me. And you are excited, yes?'

'Of course.'

'The cards told me that too. Be careful of the sun, though. Be sure to wear plenty of sunscreen.'

'Thanks for the advice.'

Colin stood up, shaking Reg's hand. As he walked past Julia's group, he said, 'Wow, that was amazing.'

'The woman is a quack,' Magnus said.

'Well, let's at least try,' said Julia, sitting down in the seat Colin had recently vacated.

'Ah, train girl. There you are. Have you overcome your trials?'

'More or less,' Julia said. 'Getting there at least. I have a question—'

'Ah, yes, the cards will tell me.' She turned one over. 'There is happiness in your future—'

'It's not about me. We're still looking for Elizabeth Trevellian. We're getting a little worried now because we can't find her anywhere. It's getting dark outside, and she's not answering her phone.'

'Ah, the starlet. Let me see what the cards are saying….'

She laid out a line of cards. Beside her, Reginald lifted a hand and started to speak, but Edwina cut him off with a sharp, 'Shush!'

'Aha, as I thought. The girl is struggling with her emotions, both hot and cold, up and down. Sitting, running, jumping, she just can't sit still. She wants to take the plunge into a new world, but she's afraid to just jump off the edge and go for it.'

'Okay … thanks. Anything more specific?'

'You will find the answer within the truth I have imparted upon you. The cards don't lie.'

Behind Edwina, Reginald was whispering something to Magnus. He glanced at Julia and gave a thumbs' up.'

'Well, thanks,' Julia said, trying to sound sincere. 'You've been a great help.'

'Anytime, dear,' Edwina said.

Julia stood up. Magnus waved her over, and pulled her

into a circle with Joseph and Xavier.

'She's down at the swimming pond,' he said. 'They passed her earlier this afternoon. She was carrying a swimming costume and a towel.'

'Let's go and find her,' Julia said.

It was getting cold outside, and they had to use torches to light their way along the riverside path. Soon they saw lights through the trees, but unsurprisingly for this time of the evening, the pond was silent.

'We're too late,' Xavier said, as they came through the trees to find the pond—now mostly ice-free—still and silent. A ring of fairy lights surrounded it, making it appear magical, but the waters were dark and untouched.

As they stood on the path leading up to the wooden deck, the door to the sauna opened abruptly and Elizabeth appeared, dressed only in a swimsuit. She clenched her fists and broke into an awkward run, only to stop at the very edge of the deck, where she flapped her hands in frustration and then sat down on the edge.

Julia pulled the others back out of hearing range. 'I'll handle this,' she said. 'You guys go back to the pub.'

'Are you sure?' Joseph asked.

Julia nodded. 'I'll bring her in a bit.'

They headed off up the path. Julia waited until they were out of sight, then raised a hand and called Elizabeth's name. The other woman turned with a start, almost falling off the edge of the deck.

'Oh, Julia! What are you doing here?'

Julia climbed up on to the deck. 'Is everything alright?'

Elizabeth looked down at her hands. 'When I arrived, there were other people here. They were jumping into the water, and it looked so much fun. But I got scared. I couldn't bring myself to do it.'

'You've been here all afternoon?'

Elizabeth nodded. 'Yes.'

'Aren't you cold?'

Elizabeth shook her head. 'Whenever I start to get cold, I just go and sit in that sauna for a while.'

Julia thought about Edwina O'Fara's words, and realised the old quasi-mystic hadn't been so far from the truth after all. Elizabeth, more than anyone she thought she'd ever met, was going through a transition, perhaps changing from one type of person into another, and this pool of freezing cold water was the threshold.

She pulled off her hat and gloves, then unzipped her coat.

'What are you doing?' Elizabeth said.

Julia pulled off her boots and socks, then stood up and removed her jeans. 'We'll do it together,' she said.

'Aren't you cold?'

'I'm freezing. I'll need a couple of minutes in the sauna first.'

'Don't you have a swimsuit?'

'Underwear will have to do.'

'You're crazy!'

Julia had never considered herself so, but perhaps she was being pushed as far out of her comfort zone as Elizabeth.

'Maybe,' she said. 'But it'll be fun, won't it?'

In her underwear she was shivering, her teeth chattering. She reached out and took Elizabeth's hand, and together they went back into the sauna, the baking hot air reheating their bones. After five minutes or so, Julia stood up.

'It's time,' she said. 'Hold my hand. No excuses this time.'

'Is it deep?'

'Deep enough, but don't worry. You'll be fine.'

Without any other people around, and in the dark, Julia's own doubts were creeping in, but this had become a threshold moment for her, too. And she wasn't about to back out. She pushed open the door to let the freezing air in, then took Elizabeth's hand.

'Are you ready?'

Elizabeth giggled. 'No, but yes!'

'On three. One … two … three!'

They ran across the wooden deck. The black waters of the pond yawned. Julia became aware of a wild howl of terror, and wondered which of them—or maybe both—it came from. The deck was rapidly receding, the pond below their feet. A chilly gust of wind rattled through the trees, inviting them in.

'Now!'

Julia felt Elizabeth's hand tug on hers, and knew the girl was having second thoughts, but she held on. Elizabeth wailed as they jumped out over the water together, crashing down with a huge splash.

The water was chest deep. Julia's feet touched down on the coarse gravel bed, her head going under. The cold stripped her of all thoughts and reason, then she pushed her head back above the water, gasping for air.

'Wowowowee!' cried Elizabeth, flapping in the water beside her. 'That was … amazing! Come on, let's have a race!'

She started swimming across the pond. Julia, still waiting for the shock to pass, attempted a few strokes in pursuit, but her body wasn't having it. She splashed to a shallower area and stood up in the water, shivering, turned to look at the sauna, just as the light through the little window in the door went out.

'Ah, Elizabeth—'

Elizabeth stood up, flapped at the water, and let out a

scream of delight. 'Wow! I've never felt so alive!'

'Enjoy it while it lasts. The sauna light just went off.'

'Oh? There was a sign on the inside that said it switches off automatically at six. Is it that time already?'

'I suppose it must be. Come on, let's get out of here before it cools down.'

They climbed back on to the deck. Julia, shivering, pulled open the sauna door, but the room had already cooled down, giving them little respite from the cold. She grabbed a towel out of a box and wiped herself down.

'How are we going to warm back up?' Elizabeth said. 'Are we going to die?'

Julia looked around for a manual switch to turn the sauna back on, but could see nothing. Back up through the trees, the lights of the village twinkled.

'The nearest warm place is the pub,' she said. 'Let's go.'

'How are we going to get there?'

Julia, sure the cold had instilled a level of madness, grinned. 'We run.'

'Run? I can't run!'

'Everyone can run. Grab your clothes and boots.'

'Aren't we going to put them on?'

The madness was in total control as Julia shook her head. 'No.'

'We run just like this?'

'Yes.'

'Wow! You're crazy!'

They gathered up their things. Julia wrapped her clothes in her coat, her boots underneath, tucking the bundle under her arm so she was able to hold her torch with the other hand.

'I'm ready,' Elizabeth said. 'Can I do the countdown?'

'Sure,' Julia said with a smile.

'Ten … nine—'

'Hurry up, I'm freezing!'

Elizabeth tittered. 'Okay. Three—two—one—'

Elizabeth was off before Julia was even ready, the moonlight illuminating the path just enough for her to see. Julia gave up on trying to use the torch and just tried to keep up as Elizabeth, legs gym-honed, tore up the grassy path towards the village.

She was panting by the time she reached the steps that led up to the little bridge over the river. Elizabeth had stopped to wait, and reached out a hand to help Julia up.

'Nearly there!' she gasped, the streetlights illuminating a wide grin.

Summoning a last burst of energy, Julia hurried to keep up as Elizabeth sprinted up the gentle hill to the pub on the corner, pulling open the door as Julia arrived.

'Wait a minute!' Julia said. 'I've got to put some clothes on!'

'Oh, yes, I forgot!' Elizabeth said.

'You'd better too, or there are a few old men in there who might have heart attacks.'

Julia had no choice but to go commando, squeezing the water out of her underwear and putting it into her coat pocket. Back in her clothes, though, she felt snug, the heat from the run radiating out.

'Pints on me!' Elizabeth said, then reached out a hand to Julia and smiled. 'Thank you,' she said, for the first time the façade with which she had arrived in Birch Valley truly dropping. 'I don't think I could have done it without you.'

'How do you feel?' Julia asked.

Elizabeth frowned, then gave the kind of smile that wouldn't have been out of place in a movie ending scene. 'Different,' she said. 'Better.'

'Then let's go and get those pints,' Julia said.

21

THE WEDDING

'Hi Mum, it's me, Julia.'

'Hello, love. Are you still going to come this evening?'

Julia looked out of the window. The skies were clear and bright, not a cloud to be seen.

'Actually … I wanted to ask you something. There's a bit of a celebration going on today, so I wondered if you and dad and … well, everyone, wanted to come up. You could bring the camper van.'

'It's not far, so I suppose so. Then perhaps we could go back together?'

'That would be great.'

'Where is it?'

'In the grounds of Birch Valley Grange.'

'The National Trust Manor House? I know the place. We took you there once as kids. I remember you jumping up and down on some antique priceless bed. Isn't it supposed to be haunted?'

Julia smiled at the memory of Lord Andrews with a bedsheet over his head. 'Yes, I've heard that too.'

'Fantastic. Cousin Albert fancies himself as a bit of a ghosthunter. What time?'

Julia shrugged. 'It starts after lunch, so whenever you're ready.'

'Great. Can't wait to see you, love.'

'And you, Mum. Oh, and Merry Christmas.'

Downstairs in the kitchen, Magnus and Xavier were eating breakfast while watching *The Snowman* on the TV in the corner. As Julia sat down and grabbed a piece of toast, Elizabeth appeared, dressed in jeans and t-shirt, her hair casually tied up in a ponytail.

'Don't get too comfortable,' she said. 'I need your help to get Mrs. Swann ready.'

'The wedding,' Julia said. 'Of course.'

Elizabeth's eyes sparkled. 'It's going to be spectacular.'

After breakfast, Julia went outside to find Joseph, sitting, as always, out with the wolves. The pups looked stronger than ever, pushing and shoving at Bella as their mother looked on.

'How did you feel this morning?' Joseph said. 'The rate that you, Kelly, and Elizabeth were knocking back the peach schnapps was quite alarming. I haven't seen anything like that since my university's poetry club's final year trip to Magaluf.'

'Your poetry club's trip to … okay, we'll hold that for now. Actually, I asked Don to top Elizabeth's drinks up with water. She's not so used to it.'

'Not hardcore like you and Kelly?'

Julia grinned. 'Nothing a paracetamol can't fix. Are you looking forward to not getting married today?'

'I can't wait.' He held her eyes. 'Do you think we'll have time to take a walk later?'

'I'll check my busy schedule. I got paired with Elizabeth in the sledging race.'

'Good luck. You've got to love picking names out of a box. I'm with Reginald O'Fara.'

'That's great. What's Edwina's prediction?'

Joseph lifted his hand and waved his fingers about in front of his face. '"You will find yourself tasting the sweet scent of victory … or you may not." Something like that, I imagine.'

'Well, good luck. I'd better get back. I have to help your grandmother get ready to marry into the aristocracy.'

Mabel was fussing over her dress and makeup with the fervor of a teenager preparing for a first date.

'Do you think it would be better if I just wore a hat?' she asked, as Elizabeth and Julia tended to her.

Elizabeth grinned, then opened an elaborate makeup box and pulled out a small metal tin. She opened it up to reveal a powder filled with pieces of silver glitter.

'Let me brush a little of this in,' she said. 'It's the expensive stuff so it won't stand out, but it'll add highlights and make your hair sparkle.' She glanced at Julia. 'Tricks of the modelling industry.'

'There's a new YouTube channel right there,' Julia said.

Elizabeth shrugged. 'Maybe. I was thinking of stepping away from the internet for a while. Maybe do some travelling. Something a little more….' She shrugged and shook her head. 'I don't even know the word.'

'Humble?' Mabel suggested.

Elizabeth clicked her fingers. 'That's it. I thought I'd start with staying in four-star hotels and work my way down.'

'You've got to start somewhere,' Julia said.

'Got an old tent in the loft you can borrow if you like,' Mabel said.

'That would be lovely, thank you. Right. Let's get you into this dress.'

Julia had to admit, that when it came to makeup, hair, and dressing up, Elizabeth was a pro. She helped, doing what she could, but mostly just watching as Elizabeth turned Mabel into an elegant, wintery beauty.

'You look amazing,' Julia said. 'To be honest, you might give poor Lord Andrews a heart attack.'

'Do you think so? Perhaps I could wear a jacket over the top or something.'

'No, you'll be just fine like that. Perfect, even.'

'I can't believe I'm getting married,' Mabel said. She turned to Elizabeth and took her hand. 'This couldn't have happened without you and your madcap plan to marry my grandson,' she added. 'Thank goodness that got called off.'

'I was going through a bit of a phase,' Elizabeth said. Then, glancing at Julia and flashing a smile, she said, 'But I think I'm over it now.' She clapped her hands together. 'Right. Your chariot awaits.'

Magnus was standing out by the limousine, freshly washed and waxed. He wore his bodyguard's uniform complete with sunglasses, and held the door for Mabel to climb in. Julia and Elizabeth, having hastily donned their own outfits, climbed in beside her. Then, with Magnus driving slowly enough that Joseph and Xavier could walk along behind in their hastily assembled outfits, they made their way down through Birch Valley to the church.

The entire village had been invited to the wedding, and it appeared most of them had come. Reverend Dennis stood outside, looking flustered, while families in a mixture of formal and Christmas-themed clothing filled the car park outside, cheering as the limousine pulled up. Julia and Elizabeth helped Mabel out of the car and up the steps.

'Is he here?' Julia whispered to Kelly as she passed her friend, standing on the steps with Colin and the children beside her.

'He turned up with the sheet over his head,' Kelly whispered. 'Thankfully he took it off, though. He actually looks pretty dapper. Wait until you see his suit. He's definitely got the Christmas theme going on.'

Instructed by Reverend Dennis, Julia headed inside. The church was full, people chatting nervously as they awaited the arrival of the bride. In one glance toward the front Julia spotted Lord Andrews, wearing a red pinstripe suit with green suede shoes. He looked like a cross between a circus clown and a children's TV entertainer, but rather than looking ridiculous, had managed to pull it off with a certain sense of seasonal cool.

The organ started to play, and everyone hurried to their predetermined positions. Lord Andrews stood, Donald and Harry Faulkner alongside him, as the church doors opened, and Mabel, on the arm of Joseph, came into the church. Julia and Elizabeth came behind them, followed by Magnus and Xavier. As the procession reached the front of the church, Julia heard Mabel say, 'Oh, Bob, what do you look like?'

'Always one to surprise, my dear.'

Reverend Dennis cleared his throat. 'We are gathered here today….' he called, and the ceremony began.

Twenty minutes later, the newly married couple emerged from the church to showers of colourful confetti. Magnus waited by the limousine, then drove them up to the Grange where they could prepare for the afternoon celebration. As they watched the car moving slowly away up the hill, Julia turned to Joseph.

'Do you think they'll be happy together?'

He nodded. 'I think so. I mean, I know my grandmother, and she's a spritely spirit. And you can tell from the way Bob looks at her what he thinks. Good luck to them.'

'That could have been you, you know.'

He gave a nervous chuckle. 'I'm glad it wasn't.'

'Don't you want to get married?'

'Maybe one day.' He glanced at her, and Julia kicked herself for reading too much into the look in his eyes. 'When the time is right.'

She didn't answer, but as people began to make their way down the path, his hand took hers, and gave it a brief squeeze.

22

POETRY AND NEW ARRIVALS

FOR AN EVENT ORGANISED in a matter of days, the Birch Valley Founding Celebration was remarkable. Everyone in the village with something to share or sell had been invited to set up a stall, so out of the woodwork had come all manner of interesting things to buy, see, and do. From an old lady selling homemade embroidered tea towels with cat designs, to a former professional draughts player who offered prizes to anyone who could beat him, a man performing Christmas songs on a mandolin, a couple selling homemade fairy cakes with bird designs made out of icing, a former cabaret performer who dusted off his old ventriloquists' doll, a one-eyed monkey called Rick, and half a dozen more.

The stage, set up in front of the main doors of the Grange, hosted a series of hastily assembled live shows, including a former school play performed by many of the same actors twenty years after its original performance, with much hilarious fluffing of lines, out of tune singing, and a couple of added battle scenes, just to 'spice things up a bit'. Afterwards came a middle-aged couple playing the flute and violin, and then the teenaged boy Julia had sat opposite on the train, playing hard rock versions of Christmas standards on the acoustic guitar. While he got a louder cheer than he perhaps deserved, Julia couldn't fault his effort, and as he left the stage, he had a grin that suggested he'd just headlined his own version of Wembley Stadium.

Julia had lost sight of Joseph during the performance, but as she went to look for him, a hiss of static came from the announcer's dusty loud speaker, and a voice said, 'And now, we have a special performance for you. A local legend of the poetry scene, Mr. Joseph Swann.'

Shocked to hear Joseph's name announced, Julia hurried back to the stage, taking one of the arranged plastic chairs near the back. A handful of spectators clapped as Joseph climbed up on to the stage.

He cleared his throat and looked around. 'Hello, everyone,' he said, obviously nervous as he fiddled with the microphone stand. 'I've never done this before, but Harry asked me a couple of days ago if I could read a poem or two. As most of you know, I have a book or two out.' He smiled. 'In fact, most of them are still out. They haven't sold much.'

At his attempt at a joke, a few people laughed. Joseph waited a few moments, before pulling a small book out of his pocket.

'Isn't he sweet?' came a voice beside Julia as someone sat down in the chair beside her. She looked up to see Elizabeth, wearing a string of homemade beads around her neck. 'You're so lucky.'

'What?'

'Oh come on,' Elizabeth said. 'He keeps looking at you.'

'He's not looking at me. He's looking at the, ah, hotdog

stand behind me.' Julia glanced over her shoulder to check that it was really there, and found it a few metres to the right.

'Do you think he'll read a poem about you?'

'Oh, I hope not. I didn't know anything about it other than what Mabel said. He doesn't talk about it much.'

'This one is about Christmas,' Joseph said, opening the little book. From this distance, it was impossible to read the title.

> *'White dustings, cool, like spiderwebs, scatter the fields*
> *A bell, hope, an angel's promise, lingering;*
> *A robin's cry, chimes, words that heal*
> *Merriment; friends faces, log fires, crackling.'*

'Oh my god,' Elizabeth said, holding up her phone. 'It's like real poetry. That type that no one can understand.'

Julia smiled. While Elizabeth was right—as Joseph continued to read, she struggled to keep up with his imagery—there was an earnestness in Joseph's delivery that held the audience captive. Everyone was staring at him, even the people gathered around the stalls ringing the stage.

> *'... and as the glasses raise, and church bells chime,*
> *We welcome home, our Christmas time.'*

As applause rose, Joseph thanked the crowd and started to leave the stage, only for cries of 'More, more, more!' to rise up and grow until Harry, standing beside the stage, waved a reluctant Joseph back towards the microphone.

'Thank you again,' he said. Then with a shy grin, lifted up the book. '*Tears and Smiles for Sunday Mornings*,' he said, reading the title. 'If you ask in Waterstones in Brentwell, they've probably got a box out the back. They might give you two for one or something.'

'Do a new one!' someone shouted.

Joseph glanced at Harry as if asking for help, but Harry clapped his hands and waved for him to continue.

'I don't—' Joseph began, then gave an awkward shrug and reached into his pocket, pulling out a crumpled piece of paper. As he cleared his throat, someone sat down on the other side of Julia. She looked up to see Kelly, a beaming smile on her face.

'Isn't this just great?' she said. 'It's like one of those awkward eighties movies where the nerd gets up on the stage at the prom to profess his love for the prom queen. It's totally going to be about you.'

'He's such a dork,' Elizabeth squealed, reaching across in front of Julia to squeeze Kelly's hand. 'But it's so cute at the same time.'

'The pair of you, please be quiet,' Julia said, trying to sound nonplussed, but inside she was dying. As she watched Joseph unfolding the crumpled lump of paper, she tried to think of any words that rhymed with Julia. *Peculiar....*

Joseph cleared his throat again. 'Okay, here goes,' he said. 'But it's still just a work in progress.'

> *'Snowfall white like a blanket sheet,*
> *Inside a stationary carriage I seek*
> *Above the edge of Countryside,*
> *A stolen glimpse of pretty eyes.*
> *And then through doors we disembark,*
> *Past the flustered station clerk,*
> *Amid the rising confusion tide,*
> *Missed, the chance to change goodbye*

To hello, and onward, 'Can we talk?
And maybe, later, take a walk?'

Joseph stopped, and looked up. 'I haven't finished it yet,' he said, glancing across the crowd, seemingly looking at anyone but Julia. 'Maybe later, when I get the time.'

He looked so awkward that perhaps Harry felt sorry for him. Clapping louder, he cried out, 'Thank you, to local poet, Joseph Swann. Give him a cheer, everyone.'

'I'm going to die!' Elizabeth hissed. 'That was so … nice?'

'Romantic,' Kelly mumbled as she sobbed into her sleeve. 'Oh, Julia. You're so lucky. I can't even get Colin to read the football scores to me.'

'It wasn't about me,' Julia said.

'It so was,' Kelly said. 'Wasn't it, Liz?'

'Liz?' Julia said, raising an eyebrow.

'One hundred percent,' Elizabeth said, patting Julia on the knee. 'You need to go and find him. We'll wait here.'

The two women practically lifted Julia out of the chair. She looked around, but Joseph had disappeared somewhere. With Elizabeth and Kelly ushering her, she wandered off in a vain attempt to find him, but had gone no more than a few steps before something huge and lumbering caught her eye as it trundled up the Grange's driveway, smoke billowing out of its exhaust.

Once, the sight of Cousin Albert's camper van might have filled her with dread, but now, the sight of the van, seasonally painted with psychedelic, Night Before Christmas themed character designs, only made her smile. She lifted a hand to wave as the camper van pulled up alongside her. The side window rolled down, and her mother, dressed up like an eskimo in a duffel coat fastened up to the very top, leaned out.

'Julia! Is that my little girl?'

'Hi, Mum.'

The camper van came to a grinding halt with a shriek of undermaintained machinery. In the front of the cab, Julia saw Cousin Albert, all plaited, ribboned beard and colourful homemade clothes, sitting next to Marigold, his similarly dressed wife, and her father, much more conservative in a thick Christmas sweater.

'Merry Christmas!' they all cried in unison, as Julia's mum opened the door and climbed down, wrapping Julia in a warm hug.

'We were so worried we weren't going to see you this year,' Julia's mum said, kissing Julia on the forehead. 'But what a wonderful surprise to have a party up here. My goodness, what has been going on?'

Julia looked up. Walking up the driveway, still in their wedding clothes, were Lord Andrews and Mabel, technically, Julia supposed, now Lady Andrews of Birch Valley Grange, or something like that. She waited nervously, wondering if perhaps Lord Andrews had some dogs or security he could set on Cousin Albert and his clan, but he simply opened his arms and gave a beaming smile.

'How magnificent!' he cried. 'Welcome to the Grange. You can park on the grass round the back. Do you have a generator that needs hooking up? Or a water pipe, anything like that? The charity charlatans and their rules won't be back until New Year. Let's party!'

The rest of the family climbed out. Julia hugged her sister, then marvelled at how tall her nieces and nephews had become. Cousins Cassandra and Ebony sauntered over, both now taller than her despite still being teenagers, Cassandra in a black leather jacket with jet black hair striped with purple, Ebony dressed like a school librarian, the costume completed by a thick encyclopedia pressed against her chest.

'Alright?' they said in unison.

Julia smiled. 'Glad you guys could make it,' she said, as her dad came over and put an arm around her shoulders. 'Mince pie stand is to the left, hot chocolate to the right.'

'Epic,' Cassandra said.

'How delightful,' said Ebony.

'Welcome to Birch Valley,' Harry Faulkner said, coming up behind them. 'The costume party starts at four p.m.'

'What costume party?' Cassandra said.

'Pound says I win,' Ebony responded.

Even as Harry shrunk away, clearly terrified, Lord Andrews barely skipped a beat as he turned to the rest of Julia's family. 'If you need something to wear, don't worry, I nabbed the key for the costume display room. No one has a dust allergy, do they?'

'Oh Bob, you're such a devil,' Mabel said, digging him in the ribs. 'And what are you going to dress as?'

Lord Andrews lifted his hands over his head. 'Woo-woo,' he said.

23

CELEBRATIONS

AFTER COUSIN ALBERT had parked the camper and Julia's cousins had dispersed among the many stalls and activities scattered across the courtyard, she took her parents to meet some of her new friends.

Her father was quickly entrenched at the local ale stall Don had set up near the Christmas tree, where it turned out he had known Don from a local cricket team back in their younger and more flexible days. Her mother, after stuffing herself with mince pies, joined a group game of Monopoly where Kelly's daughter Caitlin was in a battle with Elizabeth over the home stretch of expensive properties.

Finding herself alone again, Julia went looking for Joseph.

He was nowhere near the stage, where a group of schoolchildren were performing a nativity play. She wandered through the stalls, stopping briefly to buy a knitted hat and then a couple of homemade Christmas tree decorations, but couldn't find him there either. She was just about to go up to Chapel Cottage in search of him when someone tapped her on the shoulder, and she turned to find Elizabeth standing there, wearing a sheepish grin.

'Hello,' she said.

'Hi, Elizabeth. Did you win?'

Elizabeth beamed a movie star smile. 'I think the girl was dipping her fingers into the bank,' she said. 'Nine hotels on Park Lane? Is that even allowed?'

'You've never been a kid if you haven't cheated at Monopoly,' Julia said.

They stared at each other for a moment. Then Elizabeth said, 'I'm sorry.'

'What for?'

Elizabeth looked down, appearing on the verge of tears, then looked up and gave Julia a little smile.

'For being everything that is bad about people,' she said. 'For being shallow and hollow and vacuous, and condescending, and a few other big words I didn't stay in school long enough to learn.'

'You are what you are.'

Elizabeth shook her head. 'I was what I was made. And over the last couple of days I've been unmaking it. And it feels good.' She glanced down. 'Look at me. I'm wearing a pair of Mabel's wellies. And they're so comfortable. And you know what? They feel used. They feel like they have personality. My snow boots cost three grand a pair. I have six pairs in the back of the limousine. I got them from a company in London in exchange for promoting them on one of my channels. But do you know what? They feel so … fake.'

'What did you do with them?'

Elizabeth grinned. 'I just gave two to your cousins. And one to Mabel, since, you know, I just stole her wellies.'

'So you're getting used to the whole countryside way of life?'

'It feels … peaceful.'

'What are you going to do now? You know, we can leave anytime, because the roads are now open. Tomorrow is Christmas Day, and after that … well, life will go back to normal, I suppose.'

'I have some things I want to do,' Elizabeth said. 'Some people I need to see, to say sorry to for being such an ass.'

'I'm sure you weren't that bad.'

'I don't know. I've lived inside a little bubble for the last ten years. And it felt like it had mirrors facing inwards, so that all I ever saw was me. I want to see … outwards. See … other people.'

'Well, good for you.'

Elizabeth frowned and leaned forwards, until their heads were almost touching. 'You know,' she whispered, 'X asked me out on a date. Like, with his voice. And did you know, his real name is Xavier.'

'I'd heard a rumour,' Julia said with a smile.

'He's from Spain. I thought maybe I'll go over there for a while. Perhaps I'll do some kind of travel channel or something. I don't really know how to do anything else.'

'I think the most important thing is that you do what feels right,' Julia said.

Elizabeth nodded. Then, in another whisper, she said, 'I didn't know he could speak. He has a nice voice. I wonder why he never used it?'

'One of life's mysteries,' Julia said. She looked up as a bus pulled into the courtyard, coming to a stop a short distance away with a hiss of its hydraulic brakes.

'I was wondering,' Elizabeth said, still leaning close, as though imparting State secrets, 'if, we could, you know, be friends?'

'Friends?'

'And I don't mean like usual friends, where we like each

other's social posts and pictures, but like, old style friends, where we actually talk to each other with our voices, and sometimes actually meet. You know, and drink coffee?'

Julia smiled. 'You know, there's a really nice little park up in Brentwell, and on the edge of it is a place called the Oak Leaf Café. It does the best lattes I've ever had. How about I take you there sometime?'

Elizabeth practically shrieked with excitement. 'Oh, that would be great.'

Before Julia could stop her, Elizabeth grabbed her in an awkward bear hug. For a moment, Julia resisted, then something changed in the tension of Elizabeth's arms. What had begun as something almost rehearsed suddenly morphed into something natural, and she found herself hugging the other woman back, as though with their closeness they could perhaps share a little of the respective world experience, and perhaps both leave as stronger, more rounded people.

Then, as she let go, she saw a group of small children approaching, led by a woman wearing a jacket that said Brentwell Children's Home across the front.

'Is this Birch Valley Centenary Christmas Celebration?' the woman asked.

Julia smiled. 'It most certainly is. I think you're just in time for the sledging competition, and there are plenty of places left for anyone who wants to have a go.'

'Is that a real limousine?' one boy asked, pointing at the car parked by the side of the house.

'It is,' Elizabeth said, just as the front door opened and a huge Father Christmas climbed out.

'If you want the ride, here is the car,' Father Christmas boomed in a familiar Norwegian accent.

The children cheered.

'Are you Elizabeth Trevellian?' another asked, as

another said, 'I saw her on the internet,' just as a third whispered, a little too loud, 'I heard she's a witch in real life.'

Elizabeth glanced at Julia, then smiled.

'I am,' she said. 'Who wants a picture?'

A series of hands shot up into the air as the teacher looked at Julia and rolled her eyes, then shrugged and smiled.

'Come and gather round,' Elizabeth said, squatting down. 'After this, how about we all squeeze into the limousine and I show you a few of its gadgets?'

Leaving Elizabeth in her new role as children's supervisor, Julia wandered back through the stalls, still hoping to find Joseph. Instead, she found Cousin Albert with a painter's easel hastily creating a pop-art portrait of Lord and Lady Andrews as they posed in their wedding gear beside the Christmas tree.

'How's it looking?' Lord Andrews asked.

'Coming along,' Uncle Albert said, splashing a smear of red across a shape that to Julia's eyes at least only vaguely resembled a person.

'Good, good. If we can get it up in the portrait hall before the house opens for business again next week, hopefully those National Trust party poopers won't notice.'

'Bob, will you just hold still?'

Julia found her mother beside the mince pie stall, looking a little worse for wear.

'There you are, dear. How much brandy do you think they put in these things?'

Julia gave her mother a hug. 'Don't worry, Mum. It's Christmas.'

'What a bizarre stroke of luck all this was,' her mother said. 'To think none of this would have happened without that snowstorm. I can't believe they pulled this all together so quickly.'

'It was a group effort,' Julia said.

'It's so lovely. I almost wish we could stay a bit longer.'

Julia glanced up at the sky, where it was beginning to cloud over. Evening was fast approaching, with fairy lights all over the front of the house and around the gardens beginning to blink on, turning the celebration into a glittering Christmas wonderland.

Julia's mother nodded at a couple standing a short distance away, both wearing Christmas hats, just as they leaned in for a romantic kiss.

'Isn't that sweet,' Julia's mother said, as to Julia's surprise, she realised the couple were Kelly and Colin. 'Isn't there someone around here for you, dear?' Then, with a frown, she added, 'Someone who won't steal your car?'

'Ah....'

'Oh look, karaoke!'

Harry and Stan had dragged the pub's karaoke machine up onto the stage. As people began to cheer, Harry tapped the microphone and cleared his throat.

'Welcome, everyone,' he said. 'Thank you to everyone in the village for all your help, and thank you to everyone who has attended. We hope you're having a lovely time. Believe it or not, exactly a hundred years ago today, our little village was founded when a steam train on the old Exeter Line was forced to stop here due to heavy snow. I imagine that in those days there wasn't much here other than a few shepherd's huts, but of those stranded people—one of which was my own dearly departed grandfather—several decided to stay, and the village of Birch Valley came into being. And now, a hundred years later, another stuck train has breathed new life into our village, pulling us all together, reunited old friends, igniting old loves, and restoring a sense of community. We welcome everyone to Birch Valley, hope you enjoy the celebration, and hope that you'll return again soon.'

A series of claps began, slowly spreading through the crowd, until everyone assembled was on their feet. Harry, looking a little out of his depth, gave a nervous wave.

'Right,' he said. 'Well, that was nice. Anyway, ah, in a bit we'll have the charity auction, with proceeds going to the Brentwell Children's Home. We've got some great items, including four pairs of Gandolfini snow boots—whatever they are—a pair of my grandfather's original socks—'—as he pulled them out of his pocket and held them up, a series of cheers, jeers, and catcalls rang out from the crowd—'—and that limousine over there. Then we've got a few services, such as tea with Lord and Lady Andrews, wolf-guided forest walking with Joseph Swann, photography skills with Xavier Martinez, and, ah, a fortune-telling masterclass with none other than TV's very own Edwina O'Fara.' More cheers, some a little more speculative than others. 'Before that, of course, we'll be having our sledging competition down our purpose built slope over there, but first, I think it's time we livened this party up a little with a bit of karaoke. Who's up first?'

As hands shot up from the crowd, mostly to volunteer other people, Julia suddenly knew where she would find Joseph. Aware that the celebration would likely go on long into the night, she headed back up the driveway—now beautifully lit with fairy lights—back through the empty village, and up the hill to Chapel Cottage.

He was exactly where she had thought she would find

him, sitting with Bella and the pups inside the wolf enclosure.

'I thought I'd find you here,' she said, quietly opening the door and stepping inside.

Joseph looked up and smiled. 'I think I put myself outside my comfort zone enough for one day,' he said. 'I needed a little quiet.'

Julia sat down. 'That poem … it was beautiful.'

Joseph opened his mouth to speak, but his bottom lip just trembled and his cheeks went bright red. 'I … I've always found it easier to put words on paper than to say them out loud.'

'You do it very well.'

'Thank you. You are good … inspiration.'

They sat in silence for a while, just watching each other. Then, almost as though both were enjoying the awkwardness, they shuffled closer at the same time, until they sat side by side, their bodies pressed together. Joseph reached out a hand and took Julia's in his.

'I think the wolves will be fine now,' he said. 'Shall we take that walk?'

Julia nodded. 'Where would you like to go?'

'Up on to the hill, where we went before.'

So they did, walking almost in silence, hand in hand as they made their way up the forest path through the trees now glowing again with lights, to the lookout point with a view over the village below.

As they stepped out of the last trees and walked up to the bench, now cleared of snow, Julia let out a gasp. 'Is that the Grange over there?'

A glittering Christmas tree was visible in the distance, in a square lit up by fairy lights. The Grange, it's façade similarly illuminated, looked like a doll's house on the edge of a model Christmas village.

'I didn't know the layout of the village before,' Julia said. 'But now you can see everything. That's the pub there, and there's the train station, and … oh.'

A line of lights was moving slowly through the valley. As she watched them meandering through the darkness, a long, slow horn sounded.

'That's the first train,' Joseph said. 'I'm afraid that you've missed it.'

Julia shrugged. 'There will be others.'

As she finished speaking, a line of pops sounded, and then the sky over the Grange lit with the expanding glittering flowers of fireworks. Julia held on to Joseph's hand as she marvelled at the sight.

'What are you going to do now?' Joseph said. 'I mean, after Christmas.'

Julia shrugged. 'I suppose I'll go back to Brentwell, my old job. My cat will be missing me, that's for sure.'

'Back to your old life?'

'Maybe … for a while. I don't think everything will be the same after this, though. I don't feel like the same person anymore. I'm not happy enough to just settle. I want … more from life.'

'You know, it's only a few stops on the train. If it's okay, I'd like to come up and … see you. And you can come down.'

Julia just held his hand tight. Her voice trembled as she said, 'I'd like that.' After another long silence, she added, 'What about you? What about the farm?'

'It'll be alright,' Joseph said. 'I don't know what my grandmother wants to do. Maybe she'll move into the Grange, or maybe Lord Andrews will end up living with us. He doesn't have enough money to buy it, but perhaps we can do something. You know, I had Waterstones in Brentwell call me tonight.'

'Really?'

'Thanks to the National Trust, the Grange is the only place round here with a decent internet connection. Elizabeth posted a video of my poetry on social media. They've sold out their stock of my book already, and want me to come in for a signing. Love her or hate her, she's got some followers.'

'That's great.'

'Whether it'll last or not, I don't know. But that doesn't matter so much. All that matters really is what's here, tonight. Me … and you.'

He reached up and gently touched her cheek. Julia shivered as she turned towards him.

'You know,' he said quietly. 'I haven't decided how that poem will end. Can you … help me?' He leaned in and kissed her lightly on the lips. 'Merry Christmas, Julia.'

Merry Christmas, Joseph, Julia thought she said, but she couldn't be sure, because her heart was thundering harder than the wheels of a racing train.

THE END

ACKNOWLEDGMENTS

Many thanks as always go to those who helped with this book. Jenny Avery for her incredible knowledge and eye for detail, Elizabeth Mackey for the cover, and Paige Sayer for proofreading. And as always, to my muses, Jenny Twist and John Dalton.

Finally, for those of you who support me via Patreon, thanks very much. In no special order: Donna Askins, Mike Wright, Rosemary Kenny, Jane Ornelas, Ron, Gail Beth Le Vine, Sharon Kenneson, Jennie Brown, Leigh McEwan, Janet Hodgson, and Katherine Crispin.

And for everyone who's Bought me a Coffee recently: Sonia Finch, Joeann Davis, Allen from the US, Donna Askins, Vicky B, Sherie Williams Ellen, Hairbender, Randall Balsmeyer, Peter Jaspers-Fayer, Sam Cleeve, Cazuma, Patsy Mcclure, Brinda, GreyCynic, Monica Demmerle, Amy Thay, Cesar Sandoval, Ann Chesterton, Nova Kay, Someone, Jennie B, Mary, Richard Herndon, Claire, Ian Yates-Laughton, Jim Naughton, Rowan Anderson, Andrea Richards, Malcolm from Canada, Elizabeth M. Dykes, Rachel G, Keith Turner, Sheri

Bellefeuille, Niall Nicolson, Amelie Eva, Paul M, Laurie Jones, Aileen MacKinnon, Att, Irena, Michael Fidler, Lindsay G Cowan, Spyke, Rosemary, Marianne, Denise Nicholson, Janet, and Christine Henderson. Thank you. Your support means so much.

Last and not least, to all my readers. Thank you for supporting my books and I look forward to bringing you the next book!

CPW

September, 2023

ABOUT THE AUTHOR

CP Ward is a pen name of Chris Ward, the author of the dystopian *Tube Riders* series, the horror/science fiction *Tales of Crow* series, and the *Endinfinium* YA fantasy series, as well as numerous other well-received stand alone novels. In addition, he writes the critically acclaimed *Slim Hardy Mysteries* under the name of Jack Benton.

A Train is Late This Christmas is the eighth book in the Delightful Christmas series.

Expect more soon …

Chris would love to hear from you:
www.amillionmilesfromanywhere.com
chrisward@amillionmilesfromanywhere.net

9 798822 430867 5